CW00547777

Ulmaetor

Genoivieve, Volume 2

Martin Werner Zander

Published by Martin Werner Zander, 2024.

This is a work of fiction. Similarities to real people, places, or events are entirely coincidental.

ULMAETOR

First edition. June 2, 2024.

ISBN: 979-8224729425

Written by Martin Werner Zander.

Also by Martin Werner Zander

Genoivieve
Genoivieve
Ulmaetor

Table of Contents

To NİNMEŞAORA -

the prettiest little girl anyone ever saw, otherwise known in real life as my darling soulmate wife, Yoko Zander ..... without whom the countless hours spent proofreading would have been challenging to say the least !!

Chapter 1 : Ivy, Greenbone and Guard

Proctor Lilly wore a smile. He was one of a select group of respected businessmen in the affluent Kangas Southern Precinct, and rain or shine regardless, he relished his position, going the extra mile to ensure his deep-seated gratitude was never in doubt. Proctor rejoiced in his monopoly of medicinal supplies, in truth an honorable pursuit forged with an appropriate enthusiasm, but clandestine activities pertaining to the distribution of liquor and drugs, items strictly rationed by the austere City Administration, proved rather more profitable.

Proctor was well fortified under the Protection of the Dionysus Ivy League, an established form of religious terrorism pertinent to the objectives of that god. The Ivy, a name often heard but never written, had a mandate to convert the stubbornly atheist population of Kangas to the Pantheon of ill repute. One vehicle fashioned to perpetrate this triumph was its well established black market dispensing controlled substances. Drug dealing is the most insidious type of organization, and arguably the most effective. With a complex network, it employed unorthodox methods proven to accomplish formidable goals, and its success was unchallenged. Such is the nature of a steadfast urban monopoly.

Public opinion of Proctor as the man was good. He was friendly and social and generally well-liked, even in the less affluent but vigorous Central Precinct, not very far east of the opulent Central Agora. Here, behind the Kangas City Administration buildings, is where much of the public market area was also located. Plenty of physical evidence of this has endured the passage of time. Proctor was deeply absorbed in this position, an important point alluded to previously, and he expropriated the vast field of promise by exploiting a host of advantages. Making his daily appearances at any of a dozen public places, and that may have been a lobby, shop, café or the agora in broad daylight, he would have prepared for such a visit, a gratuitous sample available to a patron of probability, somebody in possession of a keyword learned from the dark corners of the grapevine. The Dionysus reference there should not be taken lightly. Those keywords had to have originated from the Ivy League and no place else. Recording what words were heard and how often they appeared, proved an excellent metric to gauge market response, and identifying areas to exploit or eliminate became almost automatic.

There was a deep-seated method to the unfolding madness inherent in this business, and madness could have described all the other twilight activities in Kangas, official or otherwise. The gratuity in question was a dosage, or maybe two, of an unknown concoction rumored to generate a set of safe and enjoyable hallucinatory experiences. The added side effects were relatively few, a point that was highly praised and valued, and the unexpected consequence of severe addiction was regarded by all as an additional bonus. As we may come to realize, and this is a point of fact we will more than once be apprised of, for good or for ill, the distance between Dionysus references is rarely going to be great, such is the predicable simplicity of it all. It is the absence of unnecessary embellishment that helped generate a widespread enthusiasm for the product, and few questions beyond what, when, how long or how much were ever marked.

Kangas Greenbone was the underworld guild largely in control of the staples and necessities demanded by the hard-working plebeian society. Their home base was the dense and over-populated Northern Precinct, roughly a third of the city's physical acreage, but easily holding two-thirds of total population. Greenbone dealt in the official control and distribution of rationed food and drink supplies, as well as tobacco, but a range of below-surface activities concentrated on goods separate from counted inventories. Clever accounting always amounted quite a lot. Another profit center for this black and white organization was prostitution, and there were always plenty of treats from far away cities like genteel Fered Soudron, dark and reckless Milan or bustling Ersa Calamy. Now very occasionally, and going some way to explaining the vocal dismay of many residents, young Kangatian girls, and even boys, found themselves employed in various deviant and kinky departments of appetite available. We should appreciate how intricate and carefully considered this was. In Milan, prostitution has always been a tasteless affair, in your face and predictable. Not much creative thought was ever implemented there, and nobody complained. It was the power of simplicity.

Of course Kangas had all its own official institutions as well. The Kangas Public Administration, the powerful Law Enforcement and Armory, as well as the Kangas Merchant Association, all had organized mandates to forge and guide city function and daily life at ground level. There was also the City Guard, a subsidiary group to Law Enforcement, one that employed a subsidiary set of tactics highly feared by the population at large. Run by the military-led longshoremen, the Guard was really just another terrorist group, ostensibly created to maintain civic order through the control of grain shipments, but in reality, it was more about the spread of violence and fear. Discipline for any of a thousand infractions was swift and judgement summary. The Guard had dominion over the ramparts that occupied the entire Kangas perimeter. In other tales, you may know of the city's prodigious fortification, and its frightful drop of around four hundred vertical feet into the raging torrent of the River Sodon delta far below. Unwanted people were sometimes thrown from there. Perhaps more important, the Guard was also in control of the Kangas Catacombs, the extensive constructions deep within the massive metamorphic uplift that would eventually provide an ideal foundation for the city itself. We may truly admire the geology. These conditions permitted the Guard unlawful distribution of weapons and a good proportion of the untallied grain, and a considerable business payable in the form of gifts and bribes was carved out there as well.

To say that Kangas was corrupt to the core would have been be a punchline in a Milan comedy theater. That sentiment came from a city that had long understood corruption to be commercially viable. Malfeasance shall he an ordinary component of urban governance, and smart folks will always make business out of expecting the unexpected.

The Guard, the Greenbone and the Ivy could on occasion agree to collaborate on selected projects, but truth be told they had always been and had remained bitter rivals. Collaboration did instill some peace of mind in the public eye, and along with every conceivable effort employed to maintain the upper hand, by all sides, weeks and even months would pass by with a minimum of disturbance or disruption.

This reality of guild collaboration versus gang rivalry manifested itself one day in a way that bears close inspection. It is indeed relevant to our understanding of the greater tale that is eventually presented here, though the roots of that story are already in its infancy stages.

In the summer of 647, Kangas Greenbone, Dominus Maximus of the prostitution industry, acquired one day in secret, a most attractive young woman from Ersa Calamy. She had already been, if we may say, lightly indoctrinated into the Dionysus Pantheon and could have or perhaps should have found her way to Ivy, should she ever have had the insane notion to skip Ersa Calamy and the comfort of The Vortex's monumental establishment there. She was either duped or abducted, to be frank, and neither condition may count as acceptance by consent. Coming to Kangas could not have been her first choice.

Proctor Lilly had little difficulty taking an unusual liking to her when she was first presented, and this little fact quickly erupted into a thing that begged for a equitable solution. Greenbone had no doubt expected enormous profit to be generated from this particular asset, and so any proposal that would stand in the way of that ambition likely needed to have a eye-opening price tag.

The Dionysus Ivy League made an offer to Kangas Greenbone that lays on thick the swagger of historic amounts and stamped ever-lasting significance onto the marriage. Paulina "Lin" Lilly thus became Proctor Lilly's better half, all for the mere price of a lifetime five percent royalty on all of Ivy's liquor revenues. That meant gross sales. This was a little expensive, to be sure, but The Vortex, not being very much motivated by simple pecuniary transactions, was fully on side and it was done. Greenbone would never be of a mindset qualified to appreciate the potential Lin might have as a Dionysus cleric in Kangas. The Vortex considered it a fair trade, one that would in the longer term be to his advantage. Proctor had the prettiest partner in town and the newly married couple got along stupendously well together. They spared no expense in publicizing their fairy tale relationship. Everyone in town was permitted ample eat and drink at the week-long wedding celebration and profits to both guilds started tallying up right from Day One. If ever there were a match arranged on the Plane of Olympus for all sides to usurp, this was to be it above any other, save perhaps Glasya's well-honed genital massage capabilities, skills that would go down into history for all to applaud. Told and retold throughout the ages, it set a huge precedent and forever solidified the pecking order on the Nine Planes.

Chapter 2 : What Twins We Are

Not very long into the first annual commemorative celebration of the two Lillies, the writing was on the wall for an auspicious event. It seemed almost predetermined. My brother Usain and I are born. I am Ulmer. Usain is almost an hour older, and together we dispensed to our sweet, beautiful mother Paulina more than a twin's fair share of discomfort. We totaled 24 pounds 11 ounces at birth, and if that weren't plenty, I will always remember to this day and beyond the endless crying Lin would need to endure, and the distress Proctor our excellent Dad undertook, employing his extensive battalion of capabilities to smooth things over. Usain and I were in no position to help. In the summer of 648, it would be quite some time before we would be permitted to walk and still longer before Usain would properly talk, a lot longer.

And with that somewhat dark and unfortunate self introduction behind me, I have no available recourse in my arsenal of magic tricks to do anything other than catapult the entire City of Kangas, and anyone residing both east and west of Gindy's Land a full decade and then some into the future. Although I have not been accurately apprised of the exact geographic location of Gindy's Land, I can state with absolute certainty that our time is already today as I said.

Most of the happenings have not been an automatic realization for us, that being Usain and I. We are minuscule to fully comprehend the nature of everything that has transpired, but we do very thoroughly realize there has to be some common applicability to our diligent home schooling. There is other meaning behind our general lack of going outside, avoiding being seen in public by day. I tire of lamenting over these never-ending sensations of disappointment and despair buried deep within the hearts and minds of our beautiful and excellent parents, and also of Usain's ridiculous inability to stop laughing every single time his gaze happens upon my countenance. At last I conclude something has to be amiss.

Usain and I Lilly are not what Proctor and Paulina wanted, nor what they are entitled to. We do not merit what is considered normal. We should not have been their offspring. Something went mathematically wrong. The data was incorrectly analyzed and the permutations and combinations were misappropriated. Biology got itself all discombobulated. The numbers thrown into the pot got jumbled about in some inexplicable ways. Prophecies presented to the world by the most respected augurs simply did not coincide with results. We may find comfort in the notion that their intentions were benign, but I must remark on how unrealistic it is to expect success in all facets of divination and premonition. There exist too many variables. I have alone concluded that if we were to take intelligence tests, my score would fully double Usain's and even that assessment is generous. Usain, as utterly dunderheaded as he is, additionally has been afforded the benefit of a thousand gargantuan protrusions erupting from all about his head, rather like the astonishing prominences of the Demon Prince Juiblex, but far less appropriate to his otherwise peaceful and friendly character. Usain's heart is more like Proctor our handsome, excellent Dad, but nobody would guess that just by laying a passing glance upon his utterly uncharismatic figure.

Demanding a reflection of myself against a perfectly polished steel blade, the image transmitted back at last reveals what I have long suspected. Usain and I are both hideously ugly, to the point of instilling retched disgust in anyone casting the most precipitous notice upon us. I don't possess any of the disfigurements my poor brother has so unfairly been bestowed with, but I am by no means handsome like my Dad. Usain's severe lack of intellectual prowess is even worse. He has in most ways taken a bugbear's share of all our mathematical misfortunes, and there comes a day when Usain asks me to just point blank kill him right then and there, anything to put our poor sweet, beautiful mother out of her perpetual and undeserved misery. Now of course things don't work that way and the two of us would at least need to devise a better plan, but his sentiment bears deep consideration. There are not many roads available to choose from, and one can effectively argue suicide to be the least troublesome.

Throughout these long and cheerless years, talk amongst the common folk in town has steadily descended into viscous rumor rolled into horrible tales, malicious chatter generally accepted as widespread fact. This needed fact-checking at regular intervals, if only to prevent the embellishments from going overboard.

Sadly, some of the stories strayed dangerously close to the truth. In 659, when mother wasn't looking, that incidentally being one of her recourses to the maintenance of sanity, Usain began making excursions out into the free world, the busy streets of Kangas where we never played. We missed out on so many normal things. What we very quickly found, apart from people taking no liberties and just looking away, pretending to avoid us at every possible instance, is the inevitable, fanatical taunting Usain would experience from teenage boys, especially those associated with the City Guard. These are among many boys apprenticed to the next round of training. They are tapped and will eventually be placed in positions relevant to their acquired capabilities. I must hereby resolutely declare that their acumen for sound decision-making and their acquired obedience training will prove wholly unsatisfactory. For starters, they treat us as equals, not that I consider myself in any way superior to my brother, but that their indoctrination into equating hearsay with fact, however nonsensical, and their obvious lack of intellect, their absence of impartiality, their poor judgement, and ultimately their limited tolerance, made me come to despise them with all my heart. I now worry about how and why these dimwits will eventually inherit important law enforcement activities in Kangas. I'm deeply perturbed by the general decline in public obedience and the increased violent activities across the various groups that will surely result when these fuck heads are in charge. Kangas has a bleak future under the watch of these anus-sniffing loogans. I am beside myself contemplating how normal, law-abiding folks will become mired in madness, how they'll helplessly descend into darkness, not created intentionally by these miserable twerps, but by their indifference to all matters. When that happens, nothing remains sacred and Kangas is in trouble. Nobody is safe.

I am about to devise a plan.

Usain aged 12 delights in daring penetrations of the treachery of daily life. I'm not sure what is behind this motivation. Could it be the only real challenge he has ever known? Could he be looking for redemption far beyond a coward's reach? We may never really know as we shall see.

The Boys of the Guard torment and molest Usain at every instance. The disturbances and yelling in the crowded streets is met only with mild objection for nobody is eager to attract the ire of The Guard. I am sickened by this behavior, but then again an analysis of human nature, and especially personalities common to the Kangas half-orc minority, we may begin to appreciate that things are just as they should be. How would Milan or Leipzig really be any different? We may wonder.

So, I endeavor to formulate a plan. I am horrendously ugly, I must concede, but in stark contrast, prodigiously intelligent, even if I may say ultra-genius, and not many puzzles in this life have yet presented themselves that I cannot invent my own suitable solutions for. Perhaps this changes in the next life, but for now, a broadly untapped landscape lays at my feet.

I make a late night appearance at the headquarters of Kangas Greenbone. The door guard there is a fairly typical guy whom I know named Jessop, and he lets me in. I think a 12-year-old boy of my particular intellect and background might prove useful to the KGB, as I have come to call them, and that point is made quite clear up front. But first, I require a few lethal dosages of an organic poison I have been reading extensively about. To my surprise, I am directed right back to my father's business of medicinal supplies, that apparently "organic poisons" have long been classified under the jurisdiction of our own Lilly Medicinal Supply Company. Funny I hadn't learned that before.

The poison in question is ricin, and a detailed description of its manufacture I now know can be found most anywhere. It is quite lethal, and also possess the curiosity of taking several days to a week before inexplicable and irreversible symptoms begin to appear. This is convenient because it makes a correct diagnosis impossible. Ricin exists mainly as an antidote for urban rodent overpopulation, and this is a necessary control, and I see why there really aren't many rats in Kangas, at least not ones related to furry, four-legged rodent species.

I devise the cutest little dart blower, really nothing more than a drinking straw made from marsh reeds, a common item readily available free of charge from the nighttime refuse of any posh café in our Southern Precinct. In it, I can fire a pointy feathered pin, essentially just a tiny, weak blow dart, but now thoroughly weaponized with ricin. Bipedal rats are in an epidemic stage of evolution in Kangas, and populations are set to come under attack. My new little hobby, completely in line with the amusements of any average 12-year-old boy, should help steer the opposition some way towards a lasting solution. Instilling a good-sized dose of fear into the primary purveyors of public instability cannot be a bad thing.

I set myself deep into a program crammed full of inordinate commitments. I am to conduct a series of assassinations, accomplished in secret, in the dark, and with a very quiet, simple weapon. I choose to become a serial killer. Why, you may ask? It isn't that I am a bad person necessarily, or that I have chosen a particular path of darkness. It is just that I am angry. I am also tired. I have given myself more than enough reason to affect some changes. I am fed up with this miserable town.

On clear evenings, throngs of people going about their daily activities continue well into darkness, and a healthy dose of public enterprise is certainly not unwelcome for what I'm about to do, for what is about to happen here tonight. With practice, I have learned to aim my weapon with sufficient accuracy, and I memorized the predictable patrol circuit the Guards may take. On one lucky evening, my first target is a boy I particularly dislike because he has kicked me in the stomach exactly once too often. I warned him on several occasions that such activity would be unsustainable. His droplet of pleasure each time will now become all mine all at once. I don't know his name and that helps make this method of demise a bit easier. He is hit in the right cheek and neck, twice with what he thinks must be a typical hornet sting. He slaps himself several times, hoping to locate and identify the culprit as a dead bug, but appears disappointed when nothing is found.

The second target on the next night screams of pain when hit in the eye point blank, and I have taken extra steps to ensure he does not see me. Practice makes perfect, and I must congratulate myself on the quality of my work. Celebrate the results, not the effort!

The third, a captain of maybe a dozen boys, wretches as he coughs up a little dart in his mouth. He nearly swallowed it but reacted quickly. At that moment, I found myself in a bit of a pickle, as he realized something was obviously very wrong. When he produced the tiny dart from his mouth, I didn't feign to snicker at my marksmanship, but an instant exit into the crowded darkness was nevertheless prudent. He just stood there, eyeing everyone, flailing about a busy crowd in complete ignorance of his concern. They just went about their business like nothing was wrong. What could they know?

During these same nights the torment of my brother Usain continues. There is however, a noteworthy change in the sequence of events that forces me to pause for a deeper look. It isn't that the Guard boys necessarily go out of their way to single him out to haze him. It is Usain now out there doing the taunting. He is up to something I don't want to understand, but I do see how this will end.

One night he dares firing pebbles at them with a weak sling he made by himself, lifted from Dad's arsenal of medicinal supplies. There might be a measure of tolerance evident even from the Guard Twerps, but I do not see their softness lasting indefinitely. Usain is at a point in his life that assumes responsibility for all that is wrong in our lives, especially the sadness and torment our otherwise excellent mother has been subjected to. I have tried again and again, through the passage of years, to console everyone and just accept what is. I have on many occasions urged Usain to calm himself and adapt. It has all been pointless.

On the fourth night of Usain's relentless taunting campaign, the first boy hit with spit-darts appears to be quite unwell and has a fairly unbalanced and irritable way about him. The other Guards needle this first boy into something approaching a dangerous mixture of frustration and anger, and it is clear that his condition of low tolerance could cause him to react in a bad way.

He picks up Usain by his clothes and throws him down onto the road surface hard. With his knee firm on top of Usain's neck, pinning my brother helplessly to the road surface, he produces his razor sharp dagger and begins to cut off Usain's protruding facial warts one by one. This is horrifying to see. It is his methodical way of doing it that garners a lot of attention. Horrified, people forget all of what they're doing. This is an insidious kind of torture that causes everyone around to stop for a moment and watch. The pain Usain is experiencing is hard for me to describe and the profuse bleeding all over his face has made it impossible for him to see. Nerve endings must have concentrated themselves on the bottom ends of every wart and so nowhere I know of can we find a longer list of ironies than in this one little story. The Guard manages to cut some thirty of the biggest, juiciest warts clean off

Usain's face, and in addition to the excruciating pain and loss of blood, we may predict with considerable accuracy how these surgical excisions will in no way improve Usain's outward appearance. His face will be permanently covered in blood red spots, all plain to be seen, and all in stark contrast to every other defect he had already been adorned with.

The Guard, realizing his rather awkward public predicament, begins to show his own version of physical distress. He was the first to be hit by darts, some four nights ago, I might remind you, and the ricin poisoning is beginning to show symptoms. Usain, in his heightened state of terror and anger, makes a move for the boy's dagger. He manages to unleash a respectable retaliation, grabbing the dagger firmly. Despite the terrible bleeding which afforded no ability to see, with all his remaining strength, Usain thrusts the dagger deep into the Guard boy's left shoulder. It is unlikely to he a lethal wound, but an excruciating one, more than enough to elicit an exacting response. I witness all this first hand, watching from under a nearby merchant's table, but choose, for my own safety, not to play hero at this or any other instance. Cowardice is fine because I cannot be in any way helpful. The Lead Guard's sword comes down hard on Usain's neck, administering the final measure of peace that my brother has been working so hard to attain. He is decapitated right there, right in front of dozens of onlookers.

I see neither Usain nor the two Guard boys again, at least not alive by any account. And then, as two more incredibly nervous and heady days whiz by, and mother is still barely aware of Usain's absence, I begin to diagnose similar symptoms of illness in the other target boys, and soon no longer recognize anyone on patrol after that night. These newbies cannot be anything other than permanent replacements.

One night, Proctor my Dad, Lin my Mom and I are having dinner together in Dad's store. There is no conversation. I think it is the eighth night after the last breath of my brother. Dad makes references to the notion that, based upon rumors he has heard on the street, that

Usain might have perished. I note with particular interest my mother's sudden reaction. She displays a complicated conglomerate of responses to the news, as you may guess, and in particular, as a well-trained actress is expected to do, begins to wail with a horrid mixture of sadness and relief that has clearly been in rehearsal for years.

I do not hide my disgust. My plate breaks against the wall just as my water glass smashes on the stone floor beneath me. I get up in such a haste as to knock over my chair backwards and storm outside onto the street.

As coincidence and irony would once again simultaneously rear their ugly heads, I am subjected to witness another horror utterly unfit for description supplied by mere words. Nothing I may say is worthy to accurately describe what I am forced to see, and that is considering well and properly accounting for all that has taken place in recent weeks.

Four boys, obviously from the Guard, storm into the shop with a most agitated sense of urgency and surprise. Three of them brandish loaded crossbows of the contraband micro-ballista type and fire point blank at Proctor my Dad, sitting at the table with his back against the wall facing them. Two bolts utterly disappear into his torso while the third penetrates deep into his forehead, killing him instantly. Only the feathers remained visible outside.

We may rejoice about the fact that Dad never felt a thing and was never subjected to even one second of discomfort. Mother, on the other hand, is gagged and bound by the other boy and is never given a moment's opportunity to comprehend what is happening before she is dragged away abducted, possibly the second time in her experience. I disappear into the darkness once again, miserable coward that I am, but what of it? What value would there be in making this a target of four? No, I have inherited more to do. I will not be caught. My moment is just about to enter a heightened phase, and the boys are in plenty of trouble when their superior learns of this one, not-so-small oversight.

Greenbone betrayed the ricin request. That much is clear. I must lament at my own profound stupidity. I alone can be held responsible for my father's death and my mother's plight. The one place where trust could not be guaranteed was the one place I chose to confide my apprehension. Mother is dragged by the hair into enslaved prostitution by Greenbone at last, and we recall that had been an objective of theirs, indeed since the beginning. Profits from the Lilly underground had long ago diminished to unacceptable lows, and the desired opening for the KGB to make a necessary change was at hand. In the underworld, agreements stand only as long as they can.

Recording all of it as newsworthy in early 661, so ends the saga of the famously celebrated Family Lilly in Kangas. So likewise terminates the ambitious aims of Dionysus there. Everything of solid value in the Lilly possession, from unsold goods to cases of liquor to mother's beautiful cosmetics station is looted away within the coming twenty-four hours, everything that is, except for the second son, me.

I sense there is great urgency in Greenbone and Guard to locate my whereabouts and bring me in. I am so sorry for my stupidity. I am so angry at the betrayed trust, all belonging to our sworn confidence of privilege. Kangas Greenbone had long had other intentions, and waited patiently for the right moment. I am in awe of it. I am amazed by their determination and resolve. I now no longer retain any admiration for the human race in general, nor do I predict a bright future for Kangas. I am tired, but I will rise up as I gain the wherewithal to even the score. There is nothing anyone can do to make me wish for anything better. I am, after all, just a 12-year-old boy.

Chapter 3 : The Hows and The Whys of It

I spoke of irony before. There are many terrifyingly ironies in our Lillian history and I conclude that I will never become a huge fan of such bitterness. As a particularly brutal case in point, we need to understand by what mechanism should it come to pass that my Dad, handsome and popular Proctor Lilly, duly wedded with beautiful and desirable Paulina Lin, should have begotten such horrendously disfigured progeny, and twins of them to seal the transgression?! I'm referring to Usain and myself. Could there have been divine intervention screwed into it? Was there an omen hidden in the backstory that would leapfrog generations? Do you honestly believe it was just an ordinary case of bad luck? I shall endeavor to find out.

I am currently homeless on the streets of Kangas, a derelict vagabond making due with a baseline of life support. It is impossible for me to go home as the entire Lilly property is under city ordnance. All manner of investigation is underway there. The Guard needs to confiscate all Worldly Lilly Possessions, that is, whatever remaining proportion can be curated after the looting. They'll inspect every item, however innocuous. Anything that might blacken the reputation of The Guard, or even Greenbone for that matter, must be seized and classified. It must be encased in lead, welded in steel, and buried under seventy feet of Kangas rock. If only it could be burned. They could only wish I were so stupid as to show my face there. This choice, formulated by the bona fide wisdom of treating everyone with suspicion, shall prove my second competitive advantage. Spectacular intelligence is first. Pecuniary deficiency is an immediate negative that needs to be addressed, but I do recognize how others might be similarly constrained and find ways to make due. Relatives are always happy to trade a questionable testimony for a meager cash reward.

Authorities will not find any unregistered ricin or homemade blow darts. They won't even get that everyday common delivery device, unless they go out for coffee, and therefore remain oblivious to any evidence connected with the investigation. You see, they cannot understand why three boys died in such a mysterious way, though a clever investigator might think of it. I have it all with me, and that may yet prove fortunate, for if I set my mind at ease on it, and contemplate the possibilities, I can imagine further uses for it. I must first lay quiet for an indefinite period, dare I say months.

As I am technically classified a serial killer, it is prudent to alleviate a general misconception concerning such nefarious degenerates. We conclude that they generally desire capture, and consequently elect to resume their chosen trade for as long as the game holds out. Clues are cleverly shrouded in riddles, and while this helps keep authorities gainfully employed, it also provides the perp, in this case me, ample opportunity to cover a broad playing field, maximize civic disorder and augment the victim tally. But this does not fully correspond to my objective. For the maintenance of public order, they should officially conclude I am dead. It is possible, and the longer I stay low and out of sight, the better that story gets. My position stabilizes. The Kangas Guard chooses not to publicize my status; incompetence can not be suspected. Maybe one of those dead Guards, one of the three I poisoned, in a fit of uncontrollable exasperation, killed me, threw me over the ramparts one night. It certainly might have happened, and it's a story that self-propagates, the dependable grapevine converting any plausible hypothesis into incontrovertible fact. And now with everyone involved perfectly gone, there can be no hard evidence beyond doubtful testimony to support or refute any such hearsay. A rumor that cannot be refuted is truth. I am glad for this predicament, all things considered a marvelous condition to exploit.

There is however, another course of action that bears consideration moving ahead. I can, in my semi-ethereal state, affect more death. This could have all of Kangas descend into panic, unless I were to target only Guard members. I shall think on that, too.

I am satisfied with my broad ability, at such an early age, to corral obvious advantages and hack the inconveniences. I have assembled a set of skills that will carry me through. It might be fun, upon second thought, to experiment with strategies that take advantage of the weaknesses bestowed upon me at birth. I am sanguine about the unique possibilities I might exploit. I have ideas that will take careful consideration and time to develop.

Apart from all those criminal matters, I am beside myself with grief for my beautiful parents now forever gone. I am sad for my poor brother, though I concede he is at last at peace. I accept death is what he wanted, that his entire life was nothing but one big, relentless drag. Usain loved our parents so much. He was so proud of them. Look at where that got him. Not one single person in this entire miserable, stinking world ever had the common courtesy, nor the meagerest human decency, to extend an infinitesimal portion of that gratitude back to him. He was never applauded for his courage. He was never revered for his loyalty. He was nothing but a stupid, mangy mutt, and a waste of any overcooked egg at breakfast. That's what everyone said so that's what everyone heard. It had to be indisputable.

But you and I know different. We might tally up short in knowledge of the truth so I must one day participate in my mother's reminiscence. An intense information gathering mission I will, with an inordinate amount of fervor, set myself into.

Let's begin with a broad summation of the how and the why. We can comfortably penetrate deep into Proctor Lilly's past. He was our father, born and raised in Kangas. His ancestors, my grandparents, and all details concerning his upbringing appear as normal as any other storied Kangatian citizen. There isn't a shred of evidence against Dad.

I must then, go into a harsh and bitter speculation concerning my mother. What besides nothing do we know of her background? Why was she abducted by a Kangas mob? What was the nature of her family history in Ersa Calamy? If she were fashioned to be a Dionysus acolyte, why did she not stay close to home, close to The Vortex's institution? Why was she simply not presented to my father by The Vortex himself, or officially squeezed in through the Ivy League? Not a single shred of it makes any sense, and I'm disoriented and stupefied. And this is our beautiful mother I am talking about, and let's not forget - dare I say it - she may still be alive.

After some six weeks of settling into this surreptitious existence, living on the streets in abject poverty, I find new friends in a pack of canines that roam the streets by night. They have long had me on their POI list, starting at least a dog's generation ago.

They would rarely be seen by day, a point cleverly devised for their own survival, and I quickly adopt a similar sundown itinerary for myself. It becomes a great thing to bond with this troupe, this most cautious and methodical team of preppers wary of letting anyone in close.

Dogs need names, and by the time a readjusted order of command was established, by age 13, I found myself surrounded by a team of followers bent on the art of survivorship. Dobermans and shepherds persevere with a sagacity suited to outlasting years of trench warfare. They find food not laced with ricin. They elect to kill, ignore or survey all that moves. They procure handouts from sympathetic old ladies, and are disinclined to quaff what they cannot trust.

Two months go by and things have begun to settle down. With no additional information available, the investigation is downgraded to a mere curiosity. It's a joy to glean nothing from the grapevine other than the case of the mysterious Guard deaths is closed. They seem to blame Dad, and though the motive remains unclear, the what and the how of it are good enough for everyone to move on with their lives.

Summary judgement through revenge has already ended the trouble, and no indictments for the assassination of Proctor Lilly are forthcoming. The Lillies are done and their dizygotic homunculi are no more. Those abhorrent offspring were the real cause, everyone says, and a wave of widespread pity for poor Dad becomes the next public banter. The mill needs a new seed because this thread has run out of fuel, but I am nevertheless pleased to hear good things said about Dad.

What fantasies do I now dare to indulge in, what with the entirety of the Kangas All-Knowing so hard at work, forging the best-case scenario for my benefit? Stupid is as stupid does. Thoughts of Mom consume my daily consciousness, but I take a long time to consider the limited options available for getting anywhere on the subject. Making late-night penetrations into our former place of residence, the shepherds are able to find various personal artifacts once belonging to her, evidence of her existence. A memorized scent might be useful in identifying her whereabouts, or perhaps offers a clue to to her habitual movements, all assuming she has not already, by her own free will, flung herself over the ramparts. Let's not start any sanguinary escalations just yet, though it might be interesting to find out what could happen were the general population to get wind of her suicide. The bigger question regards a full understanding of how Greenbone treats such news, so until I know more, I consider it prudent to shelve those thoughts for another day.

Chapter 4 : Raulston

A Stranger From Fered Soudron

"Open up!" directed the stern, crackling voice of a man in his middling fifties, banging on the same immovable, iron door I banged on once or twice.

"Go away," responded Jessop, infallibly guarding the KGB entrance as he has always done.

"Open up! It's important!" ordered the man again. He has long, gray, unkempt hair and wears a heavy, full-length robe tastefully adorned with huge, conspicuous eyes embroidered all over.

"What the fuck do you want, old man?" inquired Jessop gruffly, presenting the gracious diplomacy that landed him the honorable position. He possess an unexpected level of authority, but proportionate to his prestigious and highly-esteemed rank. With wisdom and discernment, he employs the power of filtration. He's the doorman.

"I want to speak to Ulmer Lilly," responded the older gentleman. If you pay attention, you might acquire the sensation that all those eyes blink at various intervals. They see everywhere.

"He's dead," Jessop offered without hesitation. "He died in custody during an official investigation. Go away," Jessop added, supplying information without being asked. This had to be the official message crafted for public distribution, and that was all the population wanted to hear.

That robed man is Raulston, the learned but not especially charismatic illusionist-wizard from Fered Soudron. Some have heard his name tossed about here and there before, and while little truth is ascertainable from the grapevine, the rumors are fascinating. The dobermans watch him incessantly. They're attracted by the sudden appearance of this curious man in Kangas, and mesmerized by the distinctly foreign swagger he displays. Raulston may be hygienically challenging and the dogs don't fully approve of the smell. The shepherds invite me to watch, presenting a situation deemed to require responsibility at management level. The dogs look at me, then look at Raulston and back at me again, as if they collude to suggest something profound.

"Go and see what he wants, will you?" I asked the boys, as politely as if it were Mother. I was rude to her only once in my life. Three dobermans and three shepherds follow the robed man to a quiet street in the eastern market area of the Central Precinct. It isn't far from the main gates, which incidentally were impassable for weeks after the incidents, but are now penetrable under strict security. The well guarded drawbridge is deployed with the interior portcullis in place. The boys well know how dangerous it can be to accost a high-level wizard, or by extension any other species of conjurer, and instead of baring teeth, they flop themselves down onto the street all around him, exhibiting a completely benign, friendly demeanor. With ears perked straight up, they remain clever and alert.

"Well, you're a handsome pack, aren't you," he mused out loud.

They all sucked in their drool and lowered their heads down onto their front paws extended out before them. Raulston took the courtesy as a hint and put his hands inside his robe, a gesture that instigated sudden concern. This put all six of them into an agitated state that had them right back up on their feet in a flash.

"Ha Ha, you guys are good. Not to worry. Will you take me to him?" he asked, and with that, the dogs eagerly started on their way, expecting he would follow. They decide to go straight south into the affluent Southern Precinct, a more direct route that would normally generate a lot of attention were it not for Raulston's sudden appearance change. He morphed himself into what looked just like a Kangas Guardsman. This illusionist has mastery over a surprising repertoire.

He and I just looked at each other in silence for a few moments before anyone would speak. I wonder which of us is less handsome. Good thing the dogs don't put any extra utility in that particular parameter, though in any visual comparison of him to me, it is hard to see the data much skewed either way. It'll come down to personality, I believe, or to persuasiveness behind an idea.

"I have heard stories concerning your situation. I am sorry about your family," Raulston began, his rough and tired sounding voice portraying a long wisdom stemming from experience. He sounded real.

"Thank you. You heard through the Ivy League?" I asked nervously.

"Yes. The Vortex believes in your ability and insists on getting you educated. You are to come to Fered Soudron with me and learn magic," he said frankly.

Thoughts of leaving my helpless mother behind without a safety net made me feel uncomfortable. This is a point I will need to get over. What can I do besides inflict more death on these people? And then the dogs consume my attention. They hit the floor, wagging their tails, panting with what comes across as positive energy. They seem to indicate unanimous approval and expect me to be decisive. I spend a few minutes with each of them, starting with the dominant member, the largest and most senior Doberman that wil reassume leadership. Adjusting to the former pecking order will be automatic for them and they won't need to battle all of that out. That might depend more on whether they're at a loss for anything better to do, but that isn't for us to comment on.

"Take care and good luck, my friends. Watch and learn about my mother if you possibly can, but never take unnecessary risk. I shall return one day to see you all thriving," I said as I parted from the only real friends I've ever known, those final words met with a round of happy barks.

I could never have imagined a better place. Fered Soudron, the second largest city after Ersa Calamy, with a population of 80,000, is civilized, culturally enlightened and well mannered. Civic disobedience is surprisingly low, even when compared to the austerity of Kangas, and the discernible tolerance for race diversity is broad. The Pantheons of ZEUS and ATHENA-DEMETER seem to dominate here, not that I have much experience related to that sort of thing, but I can state with conviction that Kangas officials have maintained a long-term campaign of disinformation. They told a lot of lies and people listened. Kangas Law Enforcement is on an offensive crusade of its own, not one based on any deliberate indifference to alignment like the druids do, but by a forbiddance to adopt one, an infraction punishable by law. This concept is just wrong.

My living conditions get a considerable upgrade. Raulston employs a cook and a maid to take care of the all mundane essentials I never used to fret about when Mom looked after us, despite our incapacity to ever make her happy. I am bestowed a modest room equipped with a desk and a bed, and prodigious shelves filled with rows and rows of books stacked ceiling high all around. Many are tomes and anthologies of history, literature, legend, idol worship and magic, all things that beckon for endless late night study. This vast knowledge was largely forsaken in Kangas.

I am allowed several months to settle in without undue pressure. I can gain some weight, get used to a socially amicable Fered Soudron, and with guidance, make some important discoveries about what interests me, and where my particular aptitudes may intersect with those interests.

By early 662, I find myself engrossed in Raulston's extensive laboratories. There are two completely separate research stations without windows, and I possess extraordinary abilities in both professions. My mind is uncluttered and its doors open to a wide spectrum of intrigue. These advantages have me committed to a prodigiously massive curriculum. I undertake schooling as a conjurer in both wizard and illusionist professions. There couldn't be a better teacher anywhere. Raulston is the only individual known to have acquired mastery in this incredible dual specialization, and he's exactly the sort with a propensity to teach.

Chapter 5 : Paulina

Exercising my growing skills in the arts of patience and discipline, I focus on gaining the knowledge and capabilities I have already committed myself to. It is a wise decision. This is not your "just fifteen minutes a day and you'll improve" type of thing. Nothing can be achieved by passive osmosis. These high level spells require weeks of concentration and endless trial and error. There is barely time to eat because sleeping is of utmost importance. Sleeping is fun. Spells demand instant memorization with no allowance for the slightest forgetfulness. I bite my nails and pull my hair out in frustration.

But there comes a day when intrusive thoughts of Mother occasionally disrupt my concentration, and while I am able to manage them well enough at first, the invasive nature of these interruptions eventually becomes too much to accept. In early 672, at a time when some important study milestones are achieved, I choose to take a rest from adventuring and a sabbatical from my studies. I'm going to Kangas to see Mom and the dogs.

It has been a few days short of a decade since I last crossed the drawbridge spanning the ravine at the entrance. Shadow Walking lets me cover the distance between the two cities in a day or so, and most of the journey is a scenic green, clean and uneventful experience.

The dogs do not recognize me at first, obviously because a generation change has meanwhile taken place, but getting close to two senior surviving members is more than enough to establish the relationship. I have never had the pleasure of seeing dogs so happy. They hold their tails between their legs, walk around with these crooked-like appendages and bark as loud as they can. They jump up and down on me and dance around like a pack of morons. I am happy to report this one good thing. If only bipedal races inherited this level of humility, integrity and noble-mindedness. We would all be better off.

The next night, the dogs escort me to one of the main hotels at the Agora, next to the City Administration Buildings. Here I am permitted a glimpse of my beautiful mother making her way between appointments. She is somewhat tired and noticeably aged, but nevertheless still as unforgettable and graceful as ever. I spend several days patiently watching and getting acquainted with everyone's general routine, especially hers. When I have her a moment alone, outside in broad daylight, disguised as a recognizable, prominent city official, I attempt a conversation. I have not been this nervous in all my life. I want this woman to acknowledge me as any normal mother should, but I know that cannot be a realistic expectation. I am intensely afraid of disappointment, but I must try.

"Excuse me, dear lady, if you'll please indulge me a moment," I started in with an uncharacteristic chic to gain her interest.

"Yes, what can I do for you? Haven't we met recently?" she asked politely, clearly duped by my disguise.

"I want you to stare at me straight on for just a moment," I said distinctly. Although she was bewildered by this odd request up front, it wouldn't take long for her to see the sense in it. I am able to switch this illusion disguise on and off in such a way that permits a direct onlooker a brief glimpse of the reality.

"Ohhhh, no ..... it can't be true. There is some mistake!" she said nervously, suddenly severely agitated.

"Mother, it's me. Do not make a scene and definitely do not mention this to anyone. It is very dangerous," I said in earnest. "Everyone must think I am dead."

"I thought so! And I must continue to think so! I'm so sorry!" she responded in a bitter tone and began to move away from me.

"Mother, say nothing!" I ordered as she backed away into what was some kind of measured urgency, a move that wouldn't generate any surprises. But she was no doubt in a hurry to leave.

"Don't follow me, please," she ordered, though I know from her voice, fear is the main motivation behind that request.

I decide to spend a few days with nothing to do but watch her in her daily activities, but I now clearly see how she carries herself with a certain jerky nervousness, as though she were constantly expecting something or someone to surprise her at any moment. I lay low, wondering what she is thinking about. Her mind must be in a major state of confusion and anxiety. I am unclear what I should be thinking about, too.

A few days later, she no longer appears in the routine that has lasted the whole month since I arrived and possibly much longer before that. I am now just as agitated. What is happening? Have I done something stupid again? Is she OK?

Disguised as a prominent merchant from the Southern Precinct, I decide to ask a Kangas Guardsman, the chief organizer of the Agora and patrol for the immediate surrounding area. "Excuse me, officer. Do you happen to know when Lin will arrive? I thought I was supposed to meet her here today."

"You might mean Paulina, I suppose, am I correct" he asked.

"Oh, yes Paulina, of course. We've been on friendly terms for a long time," I agreed, highlighting an ironic point of unassailable truth.

"I believe she makes a scheduled journey down to Ersa Calamy once every few months, something about her father, I understand. Some weird looking dude in underwear comes to collect her, and they head down into the Catacombs. That's all I know," he said, and excused himself to contend with another matter.

I find myself feeling vastly irritated, like an itchy allergic reaction, remembering the horrible time I had dealing with all those Guardsmen way back when I was growing up here. This guy seems to be on a different level, but I know it's just his official duty, right here today. On another day, in another neighborhood, or on another assignment, he just magically transforms into one of the same worthless mongrels I assassinated. Sadly, I didn't remember to bring my blow dart kit with me on this trip. Next time I will not forget.

He did however, make a point to mention that mother and the guy head down into the Catacombs whenever she leaves for Ersa Calamy. What could be the reason for that, I wonder?

The dogs have no issue with the notion that I do not intend to stay. Above all, I don't mean to disrupt their order of command. With that understood, I give my respects to my friends and depart into Shadow. I make my way back to Fered Soudron.

"Raulston, I need to go down to Ersa Calamy. My mother is alive and goes down there periodically. I spoke with her in Kangas," I confided as soon as I got back.

"I've been meaning to go there, too. We'll leave together tomorrow. You can stay at The Vortex's Monastery for cheap, and it's a really good place. All kinds of interesting things happen there. And if the Kastovina Brothers say it's safe, it's safe," Raulston said with a smirk.

"Can I be disguised?" I asked point blank.

"Whatever you want. It's nothing to me. I'm not disguised wherever I'm well known, but out in the open streets it's not a bad idea," Raulston suggested. "Only thing is Vespertine, the Dionysus Patriarch in charge there, usually has a cleric type True Sight spell going and he will see you. Best is to let me introduce you so he knows."

"What sort is this Vespertine? Is he a trustworthy type? Is he sociable?" I wondered out loud.

"Ha Ha, sociable? Oh yeah, he's definitely sociable. Do you know what Verspertine means? It means he loves to party at night. That's his name. The guy is a total wild man. He wanders around the Monestario in his underwear, usually drunk, with his fuckin' dick hanging out, asking everyone whether they would be happy to give him a massage!

But yes, he's an ally, for sure," Raulston confided with a laugh. He went on to explain, "Ersa Calamy is a wonder of activity, overpopulation and urban mayhem. The streets are fairly well kept, though. Is there any such thing as a normal city anymore? Is Fered Soudron truly one of a kind? Ersa Calamy is like Kangas but three times larger. It's huge. Milan is a bit wilder and a lot less clean. The mighty Vortex, Dionysus Grand Patriarch and Chairman of The Neutral Alliance presides over, and Vespertine handles the day-to-day management of what you might call a stronghold within a stronghold. The establishment is known as the Monestario Colossus di Debauchery, a vast spread consisting of a gigantic temple adorned with several lesser temples for what they say are specialized purposes. Who the fuck knows what that means. The monastery houses maybe a couple thousand permanent residents and allies are welcome to their own private rooms whenever they come. It is well fortified and quite safe. The grandiose establishment comes complete with patrolled ramparts on its surrounding walls, 24-hour security, and the thing is all built inside and fully enclosed within the urban craziness that is Ersa Calamy, the largest known city. Regardless of whether you're looking inside or outside from any vantage point along the ramparts, all you'll ever see are buildings in all directions, laundry hanging from windows, steam and smoke from chimneys and cats, hundreds of cats on rooftop patrol!"

"Wow, what a place! Looking forward to seeing it," I said, feeling good about this little adventure.

"Good. I have a bunch of things to take care of. How does three nights at the Monestario sound? Will that be enough?" Raulston asked.

"You know, I have absolutely no idea how much time I need. I'm on a mission to learn about my mother," I said, and with that, Raulston and I turned in.

Vespertine

We teleported down the next morning. What an impressively huge and ornate place the Monestario is! I thought the apartment buildings in Kangas were huge, and the temples in Fered Soudron, but this! What a spectacle! Staying here should be fun!

That morning we meet up with Vespertine, and to our surprise his wardrobe is appropriate to the position he holds. The Vortex also pops in to acknowledge our presence. I must admit these Neutral Alliance Dionysus Clerics are not the pansies that I imagined.

"Raulston, what do we owe? Haven't seen you in ages. You're missing a lot of great parties, and they miss your illusions," Vespertine began in his colorful, dramatic way.

"Yeah, sorry. I hope to stay for a few days and partake. I have errands to do, but the main reason for our visit is him," Raulston said, pointing to me. "He is in disguise for his own safety."

"Welcome, young man. You must be aware we know a lot about you, maybe even more than you know yourself. Our Dionysus Ivy League was a miserable failure. My guess is you want to know all there is to know about your parents," offered Vespertine calmly.

I wasn't expecting this level of forthrightness from these guys, and I must admit their integrity and candor is impressive. "Thank you for the hospitality. I am glad to make my first visit to Ersa Calamy and meet you. I have watched my mother in Kangas for a good while, and just a week ago she disappeared. A Guardsman told me she makes regular visits here and is transported back and forth by someone from here, and they leave through the Catacombs. Is that story true?" I asked plainly, again expecting something very different from what I received.

"It is perfectly correct and that someone he was referring to is me. I collect her and bring her back at regular intervals. We had grand designs for The Ivy League and therefore constructed a modest Temple of Dionysus in the Catacombs. That allowed us to come and go as needed, but not have our general presence felt by the Kangas population," Vespertine admitted quietly.

"She is shocked to find me alive and thriving. She is very apprehensive about wanting to talk to me," I confided, and a nod of agreement from Vespertine signals that this news is no surprise.

"I appreciate how hard that must be. She is your mother and this situation just should not be. I am able to tell the whole story. The Vortex and I have expected your visit, but I must warn you, in no uncertain terms, how long and miserable, and sad, this tale has become. Are you sure you are well-enough prepared for it? The truth can be more terrible than the any fiction horror or the most bizarre and extravagant illusionist spell!" he warned.

"I have lived with this mystery long enough. It eats away at me. I need to know the truth, and I've resigned myself to accepting whatever that truth is, no matter how terrible," I said, and a wide-eyed look from Raulston indicates he is also unaware of the details surrounding this story. He's ready, too.

The Greatest Tale Ever Told By One Man And All Of It Is True

"I'll take you all the way back to 640. Your mother's parents, the grandparents you never knew, were prominent citizens and businesspeople right here in Ersa Calamy. They were successful and well-respected, just like your Dad Procter Lilly was in Kangas. If the story had ended there, everything would have been perfectly fine. Your mother's Dad was however, a man with issues. He had his drinking and partying habits. He was here a lot. He also had a bad gambling habit, a little something none of us approved of, but he was hooked and he was adamant. He borrowed money all over town to leverage his bets, but eventually things got the better of him, and he found himself unable to meet his obligations.

Our biggest competitor here in Ersa Calamy is The Temple of Hades, a truly evil and ominous establishment, and one that has accumulated an excessive following. We have seen evil occasionally come and go here under our Dionysus realm, and we never worried about it much, but Hades is nothing but total darkness. The Matriarch over there is Roxanne, or Roxy as everyone calls her. She isn't fair minded at all. Your granddad eventually went there looking for support and easily found it. Roxy is fuckin' hot, and he really got into it with her. In fact, he found a lot more than he expected. He became fully consumed by the Hades Pantheon and its terrifying ways of doing things. They financed him and he lost and they financed him some more and he lost big. Eventually he woke up and realized he had put more than his own life in danger.

He was obligated to offer his beautiful young daughter as a sacrifice. The required deed was that, as a virgin, she would be forced to give birth to twins, and both would become Hades clerics. That was your mother, Ulmer. Her father did this to her.

Your mother Paulina had a powerful will and a big heart evident at a very early age, and rather than resign herself to the fate she had been programmed for, she bolted straight over here to us with a valuable magic tome she had simply stolen from the Hades Temple. This tome was necessary for them to convert her to a Hades cleric, and then she would be impregnated by some asshole in whatever fucking totally disgusting ritual they do over there. Paulina really gave them, and us, a major headache with her steadfast dissent, so Roxy murdered Paulina's younger brother in revenge."

"So I also should have had an uncle?" I asked feverishly, the answer obviously presenting no surprises. My head is just spinning.

"Yes, indeed. And that didn't do one single thing to solve the problem. If anything, it just got weirder. You see, bringing that tome over to us the way she did is an extreme no-no, and the advantage becomes ours, so The Vortex had and will never have any intention of ever returning it to them. Thank you so fuckin' much. In due course, Paulina was indoctrinated into our Dionysus Pantheon and was ready to become a beginner cleric. Roxy would never be able to accept that without another fight, and so one night when Paulina went home to gather her things, Roxy and her acolytes ambushed her, murdered her father at his dinner table, just like they did yours, and kidnapped her. She was to become an expensive, high class prostitute for Greenbone in Kangas. Banging our heads together, we came up with another mitigating ploy. It was handled beautifully through the Ivy League - marrying Proctor Lilly, your Dad, for a very big payoff we were pretty much bound to accept. The prospect of Paulina eventually becoming a Dionysus cleric in Kangas was a very attractive silver lining. We didn't worry about the sign-up cost."

"And so my celebrity parents Procter and Paulina were married, and then came their horror, my poor brother Usain and me. Was it some sort of curse?" I asked, still feverishly.

"Definitely. If there is one thing those Hades followers know, it's their curses. You and Usain were meant to become Hades followers, possibly clerics. Paulina never meant to not love you and your brother. It's just that the bitterness surrounding those curses was often too much for your mother to tolerate, and although you weren't so badly affected by them, she was, and Usain very deeply felt it. He and your mother were both profoundly traumatized by that for life. You and your Dad just generally got through it much better."

"So with my family ripped apart, Paulina, my mother is just simply a high class prostitute for Hades through the Greenbone and that's it? It seems like a pretty lame ending to me," I judged, and I notice how my head just now started spinning out of control. "Dare I ask what her regularly scheduled visits are about. This story has a punchline, I guess."

"It does, I'm afraid. We are not obligated to return the tome, and this is a point of extreme loss of face for Roxy and her Team Hades. We are however, obligated to meet certain contractual conditions to prevent all out urban warfare. Procter's business dealings had for some years fallen way behind, not unlike Paulina's Dad. We agreed to collect her periodically from Kangas, bring her here so they could perform their gruesome rituals, until she satisfies them with either a pair of twins or two singles. Layla was born some seven or eight years ago and is actively in process of becoming a powerful Matriarch of Hades, established right here in Ersa Calamy. You have a half-sister, Ulmer, eight years old, and she is really beautiful, and really talented, and so thoroughly evil she'll make you sick to your stomach," Vespertine said, and laid silent for a while.

"My mother owes them another, and that's why she still needs to come here. That's why she doesn't want me to be near her. All that evil might rub off on me. She honestly thought I was dead and so it was OK for her to see this through. But now she knows I am alive and thriving. I see how she thinks. I see, in her own way, she really does love me," I concluded, and it was my turn to lay quiet for a while. Raulston never uttered a word.

"Forgive me for highlighting this awful point, but we hope you will appreciate and accept why we did what we did. Roxy held out for the largest possible glory taking the biggest possible risk. Talk about a gambling problem. There could have been as many as five acolytes for Roxy to indoctrinate, including you and Usain, your mother, and the two newborns. By not telling Paulina anything concerning your status and good fortune, we are able to see the entire ordeal through and avoid an all-out confrontation. It's nearing completion."

An Adventure To Team Hades

The next day, I throw on another disguise and take a walk around Ersa Calamy. I look like a typical pleb out shopping for potatoes. Ersa Calamy is plenty big and busy enough to be anonymous, and it's interesting to wander around and marvel at all the activity. Vespertine was a great resource for advice and directions, especially which cafés to maybe pop into, and where I might find and how to identify my lovely half-sister Layla.

The street set aside for Team Hades has a certain character I might not have predicted. There are food stalls handing out rations of porridge to homeless people. Especially among them we see a number of destitute half-orcs and even some domesticated troglodytes. There is a grand temple with a dark, unwelcome entrance. It has a really foreboding facade. Across the street and down some two hundred yards or so is a much smaller temple, equally pitch dark and ruinous. It is unwelcome looking, a perfect evil cliché. A general unpleasantness exists all along this street, but still there is a sense of care and nourishment I find remarkable.

Noting that the entrance to the small temple is open, and wondering maybe this address is connected to my half-sister Layla, I am intrigued and find myself eagerly passing through its doors. Indeed, coming inside here is proving easier than I expected, more comfortable than crossing the drawbridge at Kangas, and more interesting than going home to Fered Soudron. Though I do not yet fully acknowledge this feeling, I am aware of the complete lack of fear or anxiety I possess. I feel a wild exhilaration inside, mostly because there is this strong sense of impending doom. I want to see my half-sister Layla. I hear she is beautiful. I'll bet she is astonishingly gorgeous. I wonder she looks like my beautiful mother Paulina, but years younger than me, my pretty baby half-sister Layla. I am filled with an explosion of bittersweet apprehension. I need to place my eyes upon this girl. I don't know if I am able to reveal myself to her, but what if she has that Truth of Sight thing happening and sees me for real? Does she know about illusions? Is she aware of my existence? Does she know she has an ugly half-brother named Ulmer?

Chapter 6 : Soliloquy

Allow me to exercise a personal prerogative once more and speed things up. We have to move this thing along. There are too many fun, little stories and grossly inadequate time to describe them. Years go by and Raulston and I have adventured. A full fifteen years have elapsed since he first collected me in Kangas and it is 677. Together we have accumulated a great deal of power, wealth and knowledge, a wealth *of* knowledge. That makes me an impressive 29 and Raulston is astonishingly old. He is immense and powerful, and to my surprise, chooses to remain modest. After all that time, you'd be forgiven for thinking that I am at last grown up to be normal. Am I to be considered an upstanding citizen? Indeed, there has long been considerable hope in my mind about that as well. I must however, hereby clearly state for the record, that what happened in Kangas, and especially all those things I got wrapped up into there, events concerning my parents and my brother, affected a lasting impression on my way of thinking. Foundations are laid that I cannot now alter or ignore. On the horizon exists a murky twilight, a gradual grimness that quietly pervades over all that I see. I saw that darkness so clearly approach during my early life in Kangas. Assertive tendencies toward that darkness, and the desire to gain the muscle essentially inherent in it, played a key role in my survival. Let me declare that this extended stay in Fered Soudron, as idyllic as it has been, has done nothing to replace or alleviate previous sentiments. My time here has been paramount in allowing me to keep the darkness at bay. I have successfully sidelined the mirky twilight while sensibly focusing on myself, on my well-being, and on the acquisition of power and knowledge. In Kangas I would have just gone mad! I could not have endured. In Fered Soudron, I am the quintessential epistemophile. Indulging my jargon, the city librarian says I am the most insatiable philosophile. I still hate all there is to hate about that other place, and everyone in it, and all things concerning it, everyone except the dogs and Mother. I will need to return again one day, but not before I am ready. Who knows what will still exist after the expanse of more years, but taken on its own, the passage of time is not placed in our hands to manipulate.

I beg you to come in close now and listen to me carefully. I need you to understand me on another level. I don't expect you to agree with my conclusions. I am not trolling for approval ratings. I just need you to acknowledge and accept that whatever I have orchestrated, and the deeds that I have done, however horrendous some things may have been, I have determined all on my own and elected by exercising free will. Upon the most diligent and in depth evaluation of all available options, given the severe constraints placed upon my life at the time, I made what I considered the best possible decisions. I judiciously selected, and will continue to cherish, those options that maximize my chance of success, and all but guarantee prosperity and continuance. It can happen, and I must make this point unambiguous, that the actions undertaken are not always going to be flowers and candy. I am not satisfied with the decisions made by Team Dionysus and its stupid defunct Ivy League. I hold the Kangas Guard and the Greenbone responsible for every unfortunate thing that happened, and for anything that might incriminate me or my family. I will one day make them all pay.

It is here that I feel the strongest urge to impart upon you another little something special I have long kept to myself. Raulston has been keeping two impressive pieces of literature hidden in his private study. I believe these have been deliberately hidden from me all these years. To me personally, by and by, day after day, the accumulating mystery surrounding these two books overshadows the sum total of all the other unknowns in the universe. I do not believe Raulston has invested himself into these as much as he should have, but we may wonder what his longer-term intentions truly are. It is possible the books are meant for nobody, that they must remain out of sight. It is possible they are meant for me, but not from anything connected to the Ivy League. I believe they do not originate from any source familiar to Fered Soudron or Kangas at all. How much Raulston knows about that is a topic for endless consideration and debate, but not one thing anyone can say will make me see this from another perspective. Those books taunt me just as a gold piece dropped on the street taunts a beggar. Those books are going to be mine.

Chapter 7 : For Every Book I Consume, Two Rise to Take Its Place

Raulston Gets Another Apprentice

A favorite trick of skilled illusionists is to embed an illusion into another illusion and into yet another, and repeat this pattern to such a degree as to literally confuse themselves. Academic grandiloquence is normal among conjurers of their ilk. When no reason to suspect anything untoward presents itself, there is unwritten permission for illusionists to assume the same as everyone else, that everything is exactly as it should be.

In fifteen years and probably more, those Two Books have not once been removed from their resting spot. I'm reasonably confident of this assessment. I have watched closely for most of the last six or seven years since they first grazed the corners of my consciousness. I am in the regular habit of Detecting for Illusions. I have placed my own Illusions of Permanency and Programmed Illusions in selected areas to help. I have acquired, to the very best of my ability, the most inordinate amount of patience. All this you may inscribe as fundamental to my character because you know, while growing up in Kangas, I learned a few things about people.

I do not expect Raulston to possess any miraculous objectives concerning those books. If he does have a pre-eminent mindset, he does a remarkable job keeping intentions hidden. In the best case scenario, there are no objectives in place for them at all. But whatever happens, I will never allow anyone to recognize my passion for them; that would only invite questions.

My appetite for the knowledge contained within these pages reaches a point of no return in 679 when a young man of extraordinary intellect pays Raulston a visit. This is a remarkable character, one whose noteworthy charisma is set to challenge mine and Raulston's both. He is surely the least handsome of us, and this repulsive charisma has its own unique roster of benefits as we shall see. His brain is tremendous, and he appears to posses a preternatural instinct for arcane magic and lore. He poses a plausible, perhaps a highly desirable apprentice to Raulston, some newish kind of Prestidigitator. That surely leaves me out on my own unattended. Despite my misanthropic temperament, the new guy might one day wish to be my apprentice, and that gesture won't be forgotten. He has the most ignominious name, one that he could not have willfully bestowed upon himself. He acquired it through some undue coercion, or perhaps by way of a curse for which no antidote was available. His name is Fred G. Gearbox, and the basis for that queer middle initial is indeterminate. He would have been at home working in the Kangas Catacombs with a name like that, but surely that could not be this same Fred.

New procedures and conditions abound, and they do render ample opportunities for me to become self-reliant. I have matured in both professions of arcane wizardry and am, strictly speaking, perfectly capable of furthering my own agenda. Let's allow that my education from now on is self-directed. Fred G. emerges as a highly compelling individual for Raulston, and with their concentration far removed from my activities, and with my long-standing illusions still undetected, I can begin a new chapter of research.

So What Is There To Stand in My Way?

According to my illusion, the books rest on their shelf, side by side, right where they have always been. But this is an illusion. The books are on my bed. This is their new home. I feel an overwhelming apprehension for what I'm about to do. I've resolved to open them, turn their beautifully decorated cover boards over to the left and, barring any unexpected difficulties, begin reading.

My power of reason is straight off a prismatic haze and my thoughts are indecipherable. I am unable to aptly describe the sensation that is coming over me. I cannot be sure which book enacted this invocation or whether it was both, but affirming their similar origin makes the debate irrelevant. I sense I am selected and unanimously elected to embark upon an inaugural mission. I have been chosen. I am the chosen one. I might want to reconsider whether this really is the power of free will. Perhaps it is not.

The lesser of the two books, or possibly just the smaller one - I cannot be certain - outlines the strategic value of and the recipe for the procurement of a biological weapon of mass destruction. It's a very simple concept to behold, and I find I am overjoyed with what should become a spellbinding hobby. This is the sort of fun my entire life has been deprived of, and since I may live life on my own account, I am ready to embark upon this sensational adventure.

The bigger volume descends into a genre of arcane magic I judge to be dark. It seems to require first a magical decipher, and it is surely not a language that even Raulston knows. It is written in a way as to lock its hold on my attention. Its magic words will probably penetrate my subconscious. As their meaning begins to unravel in my mind, and the allegory becomes a little clearer, I wonder maybe it isn't a magical cipher at all. It isn't even encrypted. It is meant for a selected individual with a extremely narrowed frame of mind. I can see why some members of the Dionysus Ivy League, or possibly acolytes and idolators of The Vortex might be charmed by this, and surely Raulston has long been singled out, slotted into that category. But this is not that. This is altogether different, indeed a whole separate realization. Here I have, at last squarely laid out before me, a window into the unequivocal truth that has eluded me since birth. Until now every quest toward such an understanding has been in vain. Broad confirmation that my long held biases are unambiguous facts compels me to adopt these universal truths as my very own. I cannot now unsee what I do see. I will never again feel obligated to reevaluate my choices. Raulston either knew about this he or didn't. If he did, was he saving it for later? I shall one day need to find out. My time in Fered Soudron ends today.

In Search of Comfortable Exile

Shadow Walking with as much as I can hold, I whisk into the night and head straight north. I have two portable holes and a large sack full of life support necessities, spell components, precisely four important books and money. I have also taken, and this will become evident soonest, a marvelous little device that will be my new home. When my absence is discovered, I will be far away. Everyone will think my target is south to Ersa Calamy or Milan, or very likely I have gone west back to Kangas, in search of Mother. There is a small possibly I am east toward Leipzig, but I definitely did not go north. There's nothing up there, except Fered Loron, the one town that would never be an attention grabber for any illusionist.

I Shadow Wander and Fly and walk great distances north of Sodon Sovany. Eastward into the Mountains of Bahamut gets me too near of giants and dragons, all generally benign, but also things to amuse myself with later. Gradually making my way northwest gets me into the flat, bleak, barren, swampy wasteland known as Cirsalsomere. It is a huge, empty land, completely without friends. There are no inhabitants because there are no resources. It is very roughly circular, and together with the cold and foreboding Marshes of Nulwong dominating a large percentage of the region, one would exhaust more than a week on horseback just to traverse it, assuming a straight line was desired. Nobody would dare take a straight line across.

Along the northern perimeter of Nulwong, where the miserable, humid Marsh meets the dusty, barren landscape, a region of rolling hills sporting five or six-hundred-foot elevations is found. While flying, I discover a patch of green vegetation on one of the hills, a site very well hidden and altogether different from any place else within a hundred miles radius. A natural spring exists here, and that may be the only source of what has fortified the Marsh for centuries. Here I find many abandoned campsites and crude dwellings, and plenty of bones from various species littered everywhere. Evidently this location has been a necessary stopping ground for orcs, hobgoblins, trolls, gnolls and whatever other no-mind passing through. Nothing looks fresh, though. Perhaps they ambushed and killed one another in succession, and this location is virtually unknown now or intentionally avoided.

This is where I shall live. It suits me. If there is one strength an illusionist may have, it is the wherewithal to improvise. Land Area Hallucinations and Illusions of Permanency spells are just what I need for expedient landscaping and for experimenting with my new regional beautification project, a discriminating hobby to be sure. These illusions will notoriously dump all random passersby into a severe state of confusion. They will be hopelessly lost and fall into my a inescapable trap. Who can then predict what sort of horror will befall them and by what method their colorful demise will be witnessed. Nobody will ever get out of here alive, unless the rumors they spread are a quest in service to their captor. That would be me. What a lovely home. What a lovely day.

Now is a good time to impart upon you details of that little trinket. I briefly alluded to having filched an item from my former teacher. That device was Raulston's Instant Little Fortress, the RILF we used to called it. It is my magical house. It weighs almost nothing and fits neatly into my bag when traveling, but holds up a spacious shelter with impenetrable walls made of adamantite. I'm totally safe sleeping and studying inside. With my array of illusions all around, it cannot easily be seen, unless accidentally bumped into, and that minor mishap will be met with an inordinate doom.

Once every six or eight weeks, I'll make a day trip to Ersa Calamy, though I have been there only once - or maybe another civilized place - for food and supplies, but aside from that, I am prepared to live here forever. I have nothing to do but study.

A Return To Kangas

On this long-overdue and highly anticipated return, I employ the most autonomous method of transportation available to me now. I teleport in, magically disguised as a Guardsman, to a quiet backstreet in the Southern Precinct, the very place that had been the source of the drinking straws I needed.

Kangas has not changed much in appearance. An impressive amount of effort has been invested into its upkeep, which is good, but I note how the general population seems to have become more bitter, antisocial and paranoid. With the Ivy gone, Greenbone had apparently begun resorting to terror to assume dominance. This was met with harsh retaliation by the Kangas Guard, and not in a way that would constitute law and order. This has became a full-on gang war that rages on. Everyone is too afraid to provide testimony or witness anything. Sides were taken all around, and while The Guard has better control over the affluent areas, the KGB holds dominance in the Northern Precinct and the Central Market. The KGB controls most of the plebeian population.

I also learn Mother is dead. I didn't ever get to rescue her like I'd hoped. She remained in a bad way and eventually let go. Rumors on the street abound, but I can learn much from both Greenbone and Guard. I employ a range of perfect disguises. Drug addiction, alcohol poisoning, malnutrition, lack of a social network, loneliness, stress and chronic disappointment a healthy lifestyle do not make, and the story is believable. I understand it did not happen here. She had been taken back to Ersa Calamy within the last months. She had become pregnant and set to fulfill her second and final obligation to Team Hades. She was not able to survive that. She died giving birth to Lorelei, another baby half-sister, set to be Layla's acolyte. This fucking garbage never ends. She was my beautiful mother and I feel responsible. I allowed it to happen. I have been too introspective. I needed to have acted sooner. I could have maybe gotten her away from all this. This is on me. But I also remember I was never a source of pride in her life, so exactly what could have become of it? Surely it would have been pointless. It might well have started something truly terrible, the sanguinary ordeal of the ages. I shall nevertheless rage on as I cannot simply leave it be. I will first get even with The Guard for destroying my family and with Greenbone for wasting my beautiful mother. They are all going down. I'm going to savor every moment, rejoice in handing them their heads on plates. They are going to meet the most horrific, torturous demise. I feel nothing but contempt for this pitiful hole of a civilization. It and all its population are nothing more than a sad waste of forty thousand overcooked rotten eggs at breakfast. That's what they said about Usain and me. I remember it all too well.

The Tularemia Outbreak of 683 - The Common Story Is Not the Whole Story

In other tales, many know about what happened in Kangas in the spring of 683, but for all the research and debate associated with the event, nobody was able to isolate the exact cause. Most people with the appropriate academic intellect judged the likelihood of a lethal plague outbreak in Kangas to be dangerously high. Aggravated living conditions, systemic decline of the vital public water supply, the worsening public hygiene, over-population, compromised resources, no herd immunity and the complete lack of a spiritual Pantheonic following combined into a perfect storm that spelled complete doom for Kangas. The official story was a perfectly reasonable assessment.

I'm here to tell you that those were not the causes. Instead, that combination created an extremely serviceable condition I would exploit. The Tularemia Plague was me, accomplished single-handedly with help from my book and an outbreak of fleas. I invested four years growing and nurturing enough vectors and bacteria to intoxicate all of Kangas. This was the hobby. In addition, and worse, as public immunity was generally compromised, and the Plague brought those levels dangerously low, I was given the opportunity to release Phase Two. Public resources were depleted and could not formulate an adequate defense against a Black Plague epidemic, released some few weeks afterwards. This ensured Kangas would experience a full 70% mortality rate. All except my dogs succumbed to the bacteria. Infrastructure was decimated and survival for the remainder would be a bitter challenge for some and outright doom for others. I handed every single one of those severely weakened survivors the heads of their deceased family members on plates, especially their pathetic progeny, just like they did to my family, just like I promised. And I am a man of integrity, one who keeps his promises. I do what I say. And that is how I left it. Kangas was utterly destitute and struggled to function. It couldn't provide the most basic necessities. There wasn't a single living soul willing to go in and help. There wasn't a single cleric or temple of worship and sustenance anywhere. It was a job properly executed, and there is nothing else I care to say about it.

Chapter 8 : A Read For All Seasons

The years are passing by quietly. I mean, at least for me they are. My home is isolated and its location taboo for so long it has fallen from memory. Not a single orc has penetrated my sanctuary. Neither troll nor gnoll have tripped a wire. Only mosquitos have suffered anything resembling a heart-stopping horror in four years. I cannot say the same for the 28,000 Kangas Plague victims. That's fine; they got what they deserved. The Plague Tome disintegrated afterwards, leaving behind no trace of its existence nor any connection to me or the Kangas meltdown. From now on, I may carry and maintain only three.

I have deliberately not submitted details concerning the other book. There is so much to tell. I might have left the impression that I ignored it. This is false. Honestly, I've taken both volumes in equal strides. I have applied my utmost to achieve extensive familiarity with both of them. It's just that the big book is - well - bigger, and is proving so much more to assimilate. I haven't settled on a workable way to present it to you. The decisions it places before the user are immense, and the ramifications of any choices I am expected to make concerning it are irreversible. There is no test run available. There is no getting your feet wet or any token giveaway. It's all in, right from the beginning. I just need to get started.

The Book, as it shall from here on be referred to, outlines a variety of topics. I like to think of it as a variety book, such works generally looking right at home on any Kangas coffee table. The content of this particular book is however, sufficiently high-brow to not constitute a recommended read for the masses. It is a hard book filled with focused allegories not open to any broad interpretation. This is not a literature class. It won't be a best-seller by any means, not least because I possess the only copy in existence, but also because Kangatians were, by their very nature, not especially deep thinkers.

Let me begin by supplying The Table of Contents. It will ease the burden and will hopefully not be in vain to attempt an explanation. There is no penalty for plagiarism in what follows so you can spare me the lecture. The book has no title that I am aware of, but its six chapters read as follows:

(1) The Alternate Truth
(2) Misanthropy
(3) Relic Lore
(4) Selection
(5) Early Reckoning
(6) An Eternal Transformation

I attempt to provide a workable executive summary for each chapter:

The Alternate Truth

Reading from the beginning is required and I told you long ago how I felt. I was on this page in my room at Raulston's. Contrasts and comparisons of the major Hellenistic Pantheons are presented. Eight major groups centered around Athena, Apollo, Aphrodite, Poseidon, Hera, Dionysus, Zeus and Hades are discussed. I am not responsible for an incomplete list, but a fair and balanced lineup of compelling arguments for at least these eight is given. What I didn't expect was the powerful magical bias this book would possess, and that bias would grab hold of the reader's spiritual consciousness in such a way as to represent a confirmation bias, a confirmation of any previous decision deliberately or unknowingly already made.

The Book seems to adapt itself to the reader, but the selection of only one of the eight Pantheons can unleash the prime power contained within its pages. I believe my version of the alternate truth in question here is a path to immortality that has heretofore not been written down, only passed along in tales and songs, and sometimes through hearsay. This is a path laid out by Hades. This is the path for an advanced wizard to become a lich, evil, immortal and undead. This is what I am signing up for.

We may now acknowledge that Raulston absorbed and understood the content of this book. His predetermined alignment to Dionysus would not unleash the prime power, and The Book therefore remained innocuous in his possession. Without question, The Book was meant for me.

Misanthropy

I am made to understand that any reader who makes it this far has no friends. For seven out of the eight listed Greater Gods, that cannot be true. It is however, true for the one that has chosen me, The Pantheon of Hades. I must concede that I have no friends. I never did, unless you count the four-legged ones. Nobody likes me and frankly, the feeling is mutual. Shall I consider Raulston a friend? Maybe he was at one time, up until our trip to Ersa Calamy together. What about the remaining survivors in Kangas? Are they my friends? I'm thinking about something special for them, some kind of holiday cheer to boost their spirits.

Relic Lore

This chapter introduces a list of relics and artifacts that span the ages. The Book, adapting itself to your bias, mentions the existence of but does not allow in depth study of relics pertaining to other pantheons. As a Hades acolyte, I can learn all about The Sword of Hades, but get no details about The Holy Avenger? That's no fun.

Among the extensive list of known items, there are two that catch my eye. They belong as a set, but may not necessarily ever be found together. I think either way, it would behoove me to acquire both. They are The Hand and The Eye of Hades, and nothing more powerful, or more terrible, has ever been conceived, much less manufactured. Taken individually, each is utterly horrible in its own right. It bestows considerable power upon its owner. Owned and worn in tandem, the combined powers and effects quadruple. Dozens of spells are granted upon command, and a broad range of inherent powers are gained. In addition to a prodigious ego that is extremely difficult to reason with, the tandem pair will bestow upon their owner a long list of horrifying curses as well. It all sounds like good fun. The Pantheon of Hades is Neutral Evil. A lich must by definition, be neutral Evil to have any hope of coexistence with these artifacts.

Selection

Selection is divided into two distinct parts. The first is to decide which of life, death or undeath is to become your endgame. I think you may already guess what my selection is. There is no Option B. You absolutely get what you choose. You absolutely don't get to change your mind. I will choose undeath.

Description here is straight-forward, but making the correct choice isn't always easy. To assist with indecision, three intricate self-help surveys are presented, any one of which may steer the reader toward a choice. For myself, it was amusing that all three quizzes wound up to the same conclusion. This is a truly perfect confirmation bias.

The Early Reckoning

I am given one last opportunity to back out. I worry that invoking a pause at this late stage will negate the entire process. The Book might disappear or self-destruct. Someone else might get a chance at it. What a horrible failure that would be. The smallest risk of a deal breaker in The Book's ways must also be considered a deal breaker in mine. I will not be plagued by apprehension or indecision. I have already made my choices and intend to see them through.

An Eternal Transformation

The horror begins.

Chapter 9 : The Eternal Transformation

It has inadvertently come to my attention that a sharp knife is a universal friend in every kitchen and shop. Whether one strives to be a superstar chef, an artisan butcher or a celebrity barber, a sharp, high quality knife is a must-have utensil. I think maybe I might like to become a sausage maker. The one and only blade in my possession is at best, a middling grade throwing dagger, and I judiciously employ it scraping off all my hair, from my head and back, from all arms and legs, and everywhere else. Getting to some of those hard-to-reach areas proves to be a significant challenge, and all kinds of dreadful little mishaps result from that. Working with this mediocre blade leaves a lot to be wished for, but in comparison to my limited employment skills, it seems about right. Interesting is how I come to deal with all the little hairs deep inside my nose, and then my eyebrows, and later those putrid clumps of gnarly hair lurking in delicate places. Deeply concerning is the relatively poor results, and after some thirty-six hours give or take, this activity starts to drag painfully on. It is agonizingly slow, and before long just becomes perfectly agonizing as my skin gives way all over. I lose a lot more than hair. I am converted into a raw and blood red flesh man as I gently bleed all over everything and everywhere. I remove an unfair allotment of body parts. Sometimes it is accidental. At other times, I feel amputations are simply obligatory. I realize some of these body parts are genuinely important to people, but I never had a good opportunity to put them to their intended use, so I gelded myself. What a relief. Getting to those nose hairs growing deep inside requires intricate surgery, and I must forgive myself, for in this art I have also not been sufficiently well-trained. I have to make due with the resources available and go with it as best I can. My nose really has few defenses, and I marvel at the amount of blood pouring down my face. At some point, it seems redundant to keep the nose at all, and when a rhinectomy is finally prescribed, I get really mean and aggressive for a bit. Losing the nose does keep things elegantly simple, though my method for carrying out the amputation is not medically sound. Fortunately, it only needs done once and, since nobody is here to criticize or offer advice, we must humbly accept what we get and move on.

Sensibilities are numbed. I cannot measure the passage of time. I am violently ill and I vomit everywhere, all over RILF and all over myself, not that it matters much. There is no one around to evaluate me or look down on me. Nobody is here to mock me or educate me like there is back in Kangas. There was. The air outside offers a brief respite, but what is illusion and what is real? I no longer know. I wander around my own illusionary wilderness for hours, but there are still some things that are probably real. I hit them and fall down. Tripping and falling often seem perfectly natural. I don't know whether I'm too hot or too cold, or whether my feet hurt. I am delusional from the pain and loss of blood. I notice with interest how the sharp, jagged rocks have been tearing up my feet. The numbness makes that easier to cope with. I do feel nauseous though, and collapse on the dusty ground in exhaustion. All I can do is lie there, in a complete daze, unwilling or unable to get up. I'm not sure which. After a day or so outside, drifting in and out of sleep, I arrive home from my action-packed outing, unable to recollect how I was able to accomplish all of what had happened or how I got home. How did I find my way back? Maybe my illusions kept me safe.

I embark on a new project. I decide it is time to boil a large pot of water. I am not hungry, and clean laundry has become an unessential value to me, but I am nevertheless compelled to boil a large pot of water. The water reaches a vigorous boil and I gently immerse my left hand and forearm into it, right up to my elbow. It is hot, and after a few tens of seconds, extreme pain begins to take hold, yet somehow it seems comforting to have committed myself to this important task. Understanding why this so important is something to immerse myself in. I am not bothered watching as my skinless flesh transforms into a deep, mottled brown. The flesh on my arm is cooking! I always wondered about how that would look. I am cooking myself and enjoy continuance in this way until my arm is well done. It is essential not to waste resources, as I have since childhood been taught, and with leftover bullion, a few potatoes, some beans and a little salt, I am able to recycle myself in a most enjoyable and practical way. Good thing I didn't get swept up into that Kangas vegan craze! Honestly though, I had no idea beans needed this much time to tenderize, but am happy to know the small amount of fresh meat I could add produced a very hearty and satisfying soup. I find it is the freshness that counts. Next time I'll consider myself the bullion and save the stock. My fatty waist parts should be good for many cooks.

With this much accomplished, I sit down on my blood-soaked, adamantite floor. Small, bloody pieces of body parts are scattered everywhere, though I cannot any longer ascertain what their origin was. It's a terrible mess. Luckily, I did happen to come across my balls and post-haste flung them into the pot. I wonder if and when I should clean all this up. Grabbing my legs by the ankles, I note how I am no longer able to use my left hand as before. I suppose in principle, it still is technically a hand. I roll around aimlessly all over the floor in a fetal position, wobbling this way and that like an egg. The final destination is indeterminate, and in the meantime, I begin to regret certain choices made throughout the haphazard course of my life. I cry like a spoiled baby in despair. It is more like a hysterical, nearly suicidal screaming than crying. You know suicide is not an option now. Screaming out loud gets me nowhere; there's no one out there! Realizing RILF's adamantite walls are sound-proof, I allow myself an exuberant outburst at my own naivety. Alternating between maniacal laughter and delirious sobbing is evidence of extreme sadness and regret, a sure sign of manic depression. But all of this helps with the passage of time. I notice my left arm and the attached hand are just exposed bones. They aren't white exactly. They are a bloody, mottled, reddish brown. A mess of blood-clotted flesh has fused itself to my upper arm bone and I'm pleased to see this has stopped the profuse bleeding that had previously occurred there. Nothing looks especially appetizing, though I am hungry, I elect to lick the wound a little. I am not really depressed.

I've made it this far in good time and in good form so reading more pages from The Book feels like a reward. I am obligated to remove all my skin. A decent percentage of it is already gone, and much of me looks like a bright red, bleeding carcass. After that comes the required liposuction. Both the fat and the muscle tissue must now come off. This process takes a week, and I find comfort in my improved skills and in the good eating during this time. It seems the healing process will be long, and I will need a good amount of protein to see this project through. Thank goodness for the supply of beans I procured, but fresh meat is the key, and so I hack away at my legs with the skill of pig butcher. I wish my beautiful Mother Paulina could see me now, boiling my own balls. She would be proud of the kitchen skills I have appropriated. I could be a useful short order cook in any restaurant, or even a meat merchant for The Assassins Guild in Milan! One day I'll get myself a proper mithril blade made by dwarves. The only problem is I don't know any dwarves. It's a just a passing thought.

I do regret a lot of choices I've made and I am resigned to spending an inordinate amount of time in total despair. I wonder whether Fred G. is still the ugliest of us. I imagine I have surpassed his low by now. But the amount of crying is surely comical, and Fred G.'s general personality would probably get a small boost were he to observe my silly predicament.

Reading deeply into the next few pages highlights a point of considerable surprise: I have no fucking spells! I have not bothered to memorize a single spell in ten weeks. I suddenly feel powerful increases in intelligence and wisdom take place, and with that comes an eagerness to open my wizard and illusion texts. This is a marvelous thing, and I report my new condition with great satisfaction. I declare that the nine full days of study I invest to get my brain fully stocked with power are the best nine days of my entire life. What a feeling! I am more powerful than I was three months ago, but I haven't adventured, have I? I haven't killed anything, and surely can't remember bagging any treasure! How did this happen? For once, I am ripe with confidence and enthusiasm.

Another stupendous realization is coming over me, both in my subconscious mind and in waking thoughts. In my sleep, everything comes alive like I have never imagined possible. I cannot describe this feeling, but my augmented intellect has allowed another door to open, a secret door previously unknown to me. I am psionic, though I cannot describe in any detail exactly what that means. I just haven't the time to figure any of this out right now.

Within only another week, there is nothing left of me but a skeleton of bones. I have no physical or olfactory sensations remaining. The smell in here must be of the most horrible rotting death, but I can no longer smell. The sensations of touch and taste are also gone, but visual and auditory perceptions are greatly improved, and I discern the slightest movement or sound with remarkable precision. These skills have improved far beyond what I had ever thought possible, and I realize the relevance of the other three senses is minuscule by comparison. I gladly trade everything for better eyes and better ears, everything in its correct proportion.

Scraping my bones clean becomes the next project to undertake, and by this time my internals are the last remaining bodies of human tissue to process. It seems I no longer require a digestive tract or a cardio-pulmonary mechanism. My sausage making discipline must now come to a ceremonious conclusion. Body temperature is similar to that of a reptile. I actually enjoy bathing in a boiling bucket of water now, finding great comfort in being clean and well groomed. A light goes on, and I am reminded how an Alter Reality spell might be put to great use here at this time. RILF is all cleaned up and everything is neatly put in its place. Everything is where it should be and I assume the smell went with it. A couple of well-conceived Permanent Illusions go a long way to supporting the Alter Reality, generously improving the appearance of so many questionable things. I love my spells, and they seem to flow from me better than they ever had.

That whole Dionysus thing is a damn joke. They can all now go and screw themselves - Vespertine, Raulston, everybody. In Hades, I have discovered real truth and profound meaning behind my existence. I have passionately longed for this. I am Team Hades. I am undead. I am a lich, abnormally hideous and terrifying. I am Ulmaetor.

Chapter 10 : Fered Soudron

This nausea doesn't elate at all. I am not especially optimistic about my general health condition, but I see an noteworthy trade-off in never having to eat or drink again - ever. I will miss certain culinary delights at some point along the line, I am sure, but I despise the time and effort wasted to locate, curate and prepare ingredients, and wash. What a waste of time. I shall never be in a state of panic for the nearest latrine. I shall never wash. My whole entire world is a filthy, stinking latrine. I can eat Banquets of Heroes if I want.

Cirsalsomere has been home for what feels like a millennium, and in reality a full seven years have passed. It is time to press on, though I expect the absence may not be permanent. I forgot to mention the hood, scarf and gloves that I snagged in Kangas, items that would allow a real disguise should an illusionary one, for whatever reason, become inappropriate. With everything I own properly stored in my portable holes and RILF tucked safely inside my robe, I am in good form to Teleport. I go to Fered Soudron.

Ahhhh, what a rush to see active civilization again! But this is a very different rush. I got used to Kangas in its destitution, and maybe a similar prescription for this puke-fest of a city is something to dig into later.

Disguised as my previous appearance aged by seven years, I Teleport right into Raulston's study. An apprentice is there with him, and it is obviously not Fred G. I acknowledge the younger as Shaman Learus, a refugee from Kangas immediately following the Plague. He appears talented. Fred G. may well be out seeing to his own agenda by now.

"You miserable sack o'shit! You got some nerve showing your ugly face in front of me. And take off that stupid illusion disguise. I wasn't fuckin' born yesterday," Raulston started with. His less than cordial greeting was not unexpected.

"I brought you the RILF. Sorry I pilfered it. If it's any consolation, the thing really served me well these past years," I said calmly.

"It seems that wasn't all you made off with. Where are they?" he demanded.

"The small one self-destructed, but the bigger one remains," I said plainly.

As I reveal myself to him, I note his considerable confusion as he sees me. Surely he doesn't comprehend the bona fide disguise presented.

"What is this? What have you become?" he asked nervously.

"I am Ulmer, same as always! But my appearance has declined so I feel the need to cover up," I lied out loud, deciding not to give away anything just yet. "You are, however looking as handsome as ever, my dear mentor," I joked, recognizing how astonishing age keeps pace with appearance.

The decision to keep the truth to myself could prove advantageous. What could Raulston guess? What could he know for sure? I shall wager he knows nothing substantial. He can guess all he wants. He and The Book did not coalesce. He started an incantation, but I did not stay long enough to see him finish it, opting instead to leave both RILF and The Book behind. They are no longer needed and anyway, technically don't even belong to me.

Chapter 11 : An Ersa Calamy Bedtime Story

Layla and Lorelei

Lines upon lines of destitute urban creatures and pathetic wayfarers populate the dingy street connecting Roxanne's at one end and Layla's at the other. Every kind of minority can be seen here. Oh, listen to me jabber! I talk like the all-knowing erudite! I only just got here, all covered up and disguised - as though it matters! I could walk around here all day looking as I do and hardly anyone would bother to notice, such is the nature of this particular street. It's Ersa Calamy in essence.

I have to sit my bone-rack ass down on the dirty stone surface and contemplate the situation I have placed before myself. My pretty baby step-sister Layla is right in there. She must be twenty or twenty-four, we'll soon know. Beside her, I suppose, stands my other pretty, baby step-sister Lorelei, for sure born in 672, and probably Layla's step-sister, too. My beautiful dead Mommy Paulina gave birth to four ruinously sick and demented progeny from three fathers and I don't ever want to be apprised of any details concerning the latter two. At one point or another, I know I'm going to have to confront this issue, be geometrically squared to it, faced with it. I will need to if I want more than I can have without a fight.

Things must however, be seen to in their proper order, and this day is one so auspicious as to count highest among all days passing throughout my entire, malignant existence. Today is the day I have endlessly dreamt about and fantasized over. Today I will discover whether my feeble preparations have been grossly inadequate, whether my fantasies are in step with reality, and what the prospects are for this miserable excuse of a family.

Looking down toward Layla's black and foreboding temple entrance, the street seems to darken. The sounds of chatter and commotion all around decline into whispers. Faces and shapes become indistinct and a strong light from Layla's place shines well outside into the darkened area, beaming bright and low all across the road surface. She taunts me, I know that now. She feels me, and I feel her.

"Ulmer, do come in, dear brother," I hear in my head. Is it psionics, I wonder?

You'll recall I was here years ago when Layla was a teen. I feel that strong sense of comfort and relief coming to me when entering this temple, better than those of the other Pantheon, and better than my own home. Dozens of life-sized statues of black rams stand all over the establishment, each seemingly engaged in a different action. They are shiny, polished and beautifully ornate, made of onyx and obsidian. Standing before me are my two baby step-sisters, decorated in their self-stylized, bikini-like ritual attire. Both possess all the visible flesh and feminine curves I could ever want. Oh why did I have to geld myself? But laying the allure of an incestuous threesome aside, pertaining to their less relevant physical attributes, I see bones protruding, skeletal hands and fleshless forearms, and ribcages growing outside rather than inside their bodies. These matters appear weird at first, but upon a detailed comparison to myself, they must be perfectly reasonable and correct. This feature is especially pronounced in Layla, though the girls appear to be in unequal stages of transition, morphing into something not unlike me. Both girls have long, shiny, platinum hair, and there's no reason to complain about that. My hair, what there is of it, inexplicably turned into a similar color the instant our gazes met, all neatly cut and combed, too.

Little Lorelei is just fourteen but presents herself with poise and maturity. She knows her trade, gently undoing my shabby coverings as

I dispel my useless, illusionary disguise. In no time she has me standing bare in front of them, in plain sight as I am. Bare bones are truly what I am.

"You must stay here with us where you are safe. These streets are treacherous and unpredictable, and we must take good care of you," Layla advised with her sultry, soft-spoken voice. "You are our dear brother, our beloved lord and master, and we exist for you, and you must see how our goals indeed align. Stay with us, for we share many things."

She runs her frigid, bony hands all over all my exposed creakiness, and they feel comfortable and warm, like smooth skin touching skin, a sensation we would have known had we shared a bed as children.

"I can stay," I said, and with that the girls start working themselves into some kind of wild dance ritual I must have read about but mostly ignored. It is a systematic, erotic progression that proves enthralling to watch. I thought Dionysus orgies were explicit, but this! Surely such activity in Kangas could never have been staged for me at all, the weenie dork that I was born as, but I know why this one is. I acknowledge divine ritual activities are new to me and beyond my control, and these skilled clerics are my sweet, baby step-sisters. It's glorious to witness.

Layla and Lorelei, hand in hand with me at my right and left, slowly escort my pathetic bone-rack of a body into a dark inner chamber, a sleeping room, or perhaps a praying room, but in addition to sporting a vast satin mattress with plush cushions everywhere, it is completely buried by thousands of brightly shining, slithering snakes. It all feels perfectly corny and nerdy and fantastic, yet somehow exactly as I had imagined.

"Go ahead, brother. They won't bite," Lorelei giggled, drawing my skeletal hand toward her and putting my fingers in her mouth.

"And neither will she," Layla added as she began to lick my exposed ribs.

I see how I might be in for something here, and I'm on the verge of having to make some important choices. Two gorgeous mithril carving knives are next up. The girls begin carving my bones into beautiful figurines and faces. My left femur takes on the appearance of Layla and my right is carved into what must be Lorelei. Gems are embedded into me all over; gold chains with little keys are attached here and there. The names Paulina, Layla and Lorelei are carved into my arm bones. Lorelei's bony fingers are delicate and feel surprisingly ticklish as she rubs my tailbone, exactly where my prostate used to be. How can she know that? It is s a good thing I am gelded, I must concede, otherwise it would all be over right now. I might have had an abnormally huge prostate.

I force myself to admit I have never looked better. Depending on your point of view, my charisma has made great strides. I should prefer to avoid hiding myself from public view, but I know that is sadly not an option. Not everyone will be so pleased. Many will not judge this charisma as a positive trait.

Not everything is copasetic, however. I don't mind all the countless snakes going into and out of me. I rather like all the bone carving. Nevertheless, I feel a sudden wave of panic overtake me. It isn't as if these women creatures were simple playtime servants at The Dionysus Monestario. These are my sisters, and all I see are visions after visions of my beautiful mother Paulina. I adored my mother, but she never once treated me like this. This was my fantasy many a night, when I and my mother were alone, long before any sisters existed, long before things went awry. Poor Usain cried himself to sleep night after night, wasting his entire life with similar sentiments. To him, simple acceptance by our beautiful mother Paulina would have meant everything. It could have been plenty for his survival.

Right here and right now, I am presented a complex sensation. My beautiful, baby step-sisters, in the exact vision and habits of my dear mother, of our dear mother, are acting out my deepest fantasies before me, without being asked. There was neither medical consultation nor any preliminary health check. They just know.

"I must go now," I let myself suddenly say. I have no concept of fact that five entire days and nights have passed.

"Oh, but dear brother, you just got here! You mustn't go now. We have so much more," cried Layla, just as Lorelei continued to lick my tailbone. That is such a nice touch. These baby-sister clerics have unexpected influence over all undead, and that must by extension include me for reasons other than the simple family connection, but taken together with our deeply personal, filial attachment, I conclude I am at a significant disadvantage in their presence. This is hard for me to accept.

I jerk myself away just a little abruptly, deciding it is time to leave. A sudden wave of something approaching disgust overtakes me, and I am very sorry for this sentiment, but you must see how I cannot be in complete control of all my senses. As I move away from their plush tabernacle of Hades worship, Layla and Lorelei, as remarkable and inviting as they appear, sprawled all over the bed, suddenly conjure a herd of black spirit rams running from their statues all over the temple. They bite and push and lock horns, and I see now why my greatest weakness is underestimating what powers my sisters have at their disposal, what influence they might exert to counter my lame-assed choices. I am strongly compelled to stay. Leaving is simply not an option.

"Brother, don't leave. We mean you no discomfort. We love you. You must stay with us, and love us, and baby us, for together, we can challenge Dionysus supremacy in Ersa Calamy, and challenge Roxanne's dominance in our own Pantheon," Layla confided, as though engaging their full-frontal attack by Holy Symbol weren't to be understood as anything antagonistic.

"Lorelei, Layla, it seems I incorrectly assume Roxanne is your mentor, your beloved teacher and trusted guide. I see how perhaps family can overpower all, that we are unavoidably bound to one another. You must let me leave for now. I have a very busy agenda and I must think now on what we are to do, as a family," I explained. All I see are confused and irritated faces, and I know that they are not placed in an adequate frame of mind to acquiesce to my logic. I have no choice but to make it clear to them I am also the wrong person to underestimate. "Girls, my sweetnesses, accept what I say. I shall return." And with that, I Teleport out.

Roxanne

I am so glad to get out of there. My sisters are greater villains than I! It is hard for me to admit, but accepting it is my strength. They are who they are and the very few terrible choices presented to them were not easy to make.

Standing out on the street is not safe, and an illusion disguise is required to ward off unwelcome public interest. Don't make me do something terrible out in broad daylight! This is not my strongest element, and I'm certainly not in my moment to shine.

Standing on the brackish street outside Roxy's the very next day, I dart inside the establishment, unwilling to give my sisters any premature hint of my presence. This place is huge, not over-the-top colossally huge like The Vortex's Monestario, but big in a relevant way and pertinent to its status. It's blacker than coal but, by virtue of its perfectly polished obsidian, casts remarkable images back, providing true-to-life reflections of everything - all in black. It's beautiful. A dozen or more columns a meter in diameter rise forty feet up, and torchlight flickers in the beautifully ornate, shiny blackness everywhere. It's mesmerizing, and hard to establish exactly where you are relative to anything else. Onyx statues of the ram become clearly visible everywhere just when the hall's tranquility is impeded by a glorious feminine voice.

"I have wondered when you might come," Roxy began. Her beauty is remarkable, and I wonder whether my own beautiful mother Paulina is superseded at last. Roxy is human, and her perfect olive skin makes a satisfying reflection and contrast against all the smooth, shining black obsidian and flickering firelight all over the cavernous room. She appears so much younger than I expected.

"I was hoping to come earlier, but spent several days down the street," I admitted. I cannot be sure whether my response came across as jest or frustration, but I know that anything I say here will be taken however it may.

"You might wish to reconsider your position with your sisters. They are not exactly as they seem, and could ultimately prove to use and abuse you only for their own gain," Roxy advised.

"But you are their mentor, guide and learned teacher, are you not? You are Grand Matriarch, are you not? Surely nobody in this pantheon can stray far from your divine will!" I stated, as cleverly as I dared. I feel myself now falling for her, though I completely recognize anything she may warn about my sisters could easily be projected backwards. Roxanne is not the sum of Layla and Lorelei. She is the heart and soul of the Pantheon of Hades, and I am a complete wretch in her presence, a moron, and if I needed to urinate, I would lose it right here and now. I am falling for Roxy, just as anyone would expect. It is her game and she controls it. I am not the first to fall in love with Roxy. I love her name. I love her long, dark, shiny hair. I find I prefer rich brunettes to platinum blondes. I love Roxy's bright and cheerful smile. She is so inviting. I love her beautiful tits, and her flawless skin. I am sinking into a world my charming but doubtful baby step-sisters would not equal. My beautiful mother may now rest in peace, but will she?.

"I thank you for your patronage, Ulmer. I see how you are wise beyond any usual cleric's understanding. Please come inside my sanctuary," she said calmly, as we walked into the next room.

I felt a dozen spirits from those Onyx Ram statues line up side by side and follow us in, barring an escape. Leaving here by any conventional method could not happen without consent, or a really big fight. How liberating it is to have the ultimate discipline at my immediate disposal! Permission is by no means essential!

"It's beautiful. I feel comfortable here. This is a backless, circular stage where everyone here can witness exactly as it happens?" I asked sheepishly, pointing to the large, cylindrical stage dominating the center of the room. It is open on all sides.

"Wouldn't you like to see your mother again, Ulmer? She died right here giving birth to that little abomination Lorelei in late 672. Paulina's spirit remains in my temple for her own safety. She must never be permitted a return to Dionysus. I am forever at odds with The Vortex over this matter. We can discuss as much about that as you are comfortable with, Ulmer," Roxy said plainly, and I see how she might be alluding to something I cannot possibly be well-prepared for.

"May I address you as Roxy? I assume that name is informal. Can you bring Paulina back?" I asked bluntly.

"Yes, Ulmer and yes, again. I'm not a nay-sayer. I can do anything you like. I can be whatever you want. I imagine your sisters said exactly that," Roxy jested, though I know that considering she and I together as a team, there cannot be many things outside the realm of possibility. I am contemplating what to do, and I must be very careful because Roxy is who she is, and this is a case of blood and power versus common sense and power.

"Roxy, I heard a story about my grandfather, Paulina's dad. I heard a story about a gambling habit and a philandering habit, and how badly it all ended. I heard about how my mother was abducted to Kangas. Is it true," I asked, expecting a rebuttal or a new version.

"Sounds about right. I had to have your granddad and your Mom's brother killed. It put a lot of people out of their misery. Layla doesn't know it, but Paulina's mother is alive. She is safe right here with me. I can bring your Mom back, if you want her," explained Roxy, and I am utterly hooked. I am completely and irrevocably smitten by Roxanne, and it doesn't take a learned Sage to predict the problems that are coming as a result of this unwanted infatuation. She finished up with a real shocker, "Be careful of what you wish for, Ulmer. Things are rarely as we expect."

"I want to say 'Yes! Yes! Yes!', but I just need a little time to think. Is it OK?" I asked, and with that mutual agreement, I was permitted out the back door to keep the public attention low.

I come to realize now how I am not in complete control of everything. There are other entities with influence at play, and I wonder whether I control anything at all. Why are Layla and Lorelei choosing the same uncertain path that I have chosen? Are they determined to win me over, to stand by me, to exist as a family power entity for an eternity? I see them, honestly I do, but surely they must recognize the delicacy in the path they have chosen. There is a gaping chasm in their logic that cannot be easily filled. How do I deem it sensible to be a Cleric of Hades and an Undead Lich at the same time? We must suffer that overwhelming disadvantage around Roxanne, just as I do around my step-sisters. The girls have that over me, but Roxy has it over us all. I am only now grasping the broad profundity of this. In Kangas, there was never any kind of spiritual existence and I was raised without any such alignment. We all were and this concept is new, at least to me. Roxanne has deliberately chosen her own path as adroitly as anyone in her position would. She remains whole and wholesome. She is human, and beautiful. She is The Grand Matriarch of Hades. She is my Mistress. For my own sake, I must concede to her and let her be my Mistress. No matter what nonsense Layla and Lorelei, my pretty, baby step-sisters, may burn into their pea-brained little heads, they will always face this impediment whenever Roxanne is present. There will always be this insurmountable obstacle. I acknowledge my own choices have had their limitations presented and I need a little time to think all this through.

Chapter 12 : Tansiméta

The past week in Ersa Calamy and Fered Soudron was the urban vacation of dreams. But now I need to get away from it all, from all the vacationing that is, and realign my thought processes with meaningful and achievable objectives.

Memories of The Book have not subsided. I often wish I had it with me, and while there can be no dispute about my grasp of its capabilities, I was forced to concede one major privilege, just one. There is one more detail to look into, a trump decision held within those pages pertaining to Artifacts and Relics. I know what I want and I know where it is, sort of. But the simplicity of it ends there.

Followers lurking in the shadows might have at some point been introduced to a place called The Tunnels of Blood. I can live without its cliché name and admit its location is only roughly penciled into my cognitive world database, but to make improvements into geographic acumen, there are several resources at my disposal, most fundamentally the Fered Soudron Public Library. Not a lot of research is required to become acquainted with what I need, and within a few short days of enjoyable reading, I discover that Raulston, Fred Fucking G. and Mr. Shaman Learus have closed shop, packed up and moved to Milan. Surely that was a monstrous ambition that required an Alter Reality to affect. They must have had a Dionysus-infused epiphany, that taking a big, hearty piss in the river at the shores of Milan would become diluted tap water in Fered Soudron a few days later. I apologize for my bitterness and bizarre introspection but that is precisely how things are.

I cannot pinpoint a named location farther east than Leipzig, and since I've never even been to Leipzig, I need to allow for an unscheduled holiday extension. I aim for the famed military-based urban melting pot of 40,000, the largest city east of the great divide. It has the same population as Kangas used to have, but spread across a much more manageable density. Space is needed for organized activities here. I Teleport successfully, some forty to forty-five marching days distant, and marvel at how refreshing a new country visit can be for my productive spirit. Unlike the western cities where the architects generally prescribed a whorraled town center encircling an agora, some hundreds of meters across, Leipzig was designed rather more angular and grid-like. A series of long and wide parallel boulevards, each close to a mile in length, stop near major gates at east and west ends. Plenty of guard stations exist around these gates, and for security everyone is carefully screened and vetted. Along the enormous Central Boulevard, anchor establishments such as Father Elitch's Temple of Athena and Kalaringus Tell's Villa can easily be located. These two I know will one day stand in my way. On the plus, some of the finest steel is forged in Leipzig by both dwarves and men actively collaborating in this activity, and with the enormous mountains and endless forests nearby, plenty of natural resources exist to be exploited.

Getting closer to the purpose at hand, I decide Shadow Walking for a day the best way complete the one-week distance from Leipzig to the Tunnels. The journey is mostly forgettable, for days without end, just a flat barren land that is sparsely forested. Considering the amount of debris lying around everywhere, you might guess at a lot of military activity taking place here and there, though that sort of thing never makes my news feed because of its irrelevance. As you might also recall, I stopped worrying about the passage of time, and so the exact date eludes me, but it is early May, 686 when I arrive at what appear to be two heavily used but now deserted front entrances to tunnels going deep inside a massive mountain of nothing but rock.

These old and weathered mountains rise up abruptly from the flats, forming a fairly vertical rock wall facing southwest. The land has been substantially eroded here, especially by war-mongers, and I cannot imagine anyone deliberately choosing to live here, except maybe me. I like it fine. It reminds me of Cirsalsomere, though the deal breaker is that this spot is much less private. Two prominent cave entrances are found here, right at ground level, and no effort to conceal them has ever been apparent. According to my research, the left entrance goes into a 10-foot high, 15-foot wide corridor, manufactured to last an eternity and maintenance was therefore neglected a long time ago. It penetrates just thirty feet, turns sharply left, and from there makes a semi-circular arc ninety degrees to the northeast, opening up into the infamous Gem Room everyone whispers about but nobody ever understands.

Oh, what an incredible sight! There are thousands of beautifully glittering items piled high in this thirty by forty-foot room, all ripe for the picking! But are they really? Rumors suggest a great frustration lurks in making any greedy attempts here. There must be another function worth a deeper look, but I understand I am not the first one to come here with a foolproof mission, a carefully considered plan to walk out with all that is desired.

Wide open, arched stone doorways are evident at both ends of the Gem Room, and Shadow Walking into the next corridor gets me close to my intended destination.

I arrive at the room of the Oracle Lady Tansiméta.

This room is relatively more elegant than the rest of the dungeon, though I wouldn't say it's bursting with luxury or ornate craftsmanship. It's fairly rustic. Stone arches exist all around, and there are alters displaying a range of mysterious paraphernalia all over. Dominating the main floor of the room is a shallow, circular pool with little fountains spurting water and a fair bit of booty submerged inside, probably bribes and offerings that had limited success. In the center of the pool is a smooth circular platform onto which my excellent imagination guides me.

"Feel free to ask for what I may grant you ?" instructed the middle-aged female figure, standing on the platform in a ceremonial costume, roughly as expected. Her arms are spread out with hands at waist height, palms facing behind her.

"Lady Tansiméta, I have come looking for two specific items," I responded, trying not to seem too arrogant or greedy.

"So you're here either for personal gain or by order from someone else?" the oracle asked plainly. Even in the darkness, her crown seems to sparkle.

"Personal. These things will help me achieve my objectives," I responded as plainly as I could. The Book advised that honesty and forthrightness with the oracle was the best policy.

"I appreciate your candor. It makes things simpler," Tansiméta reported. "Travelers always come here tied up with complications," she added.

"Thank you. I received good advice," I admitted, though I cannot be sure what made me disclose that. I learned some valuable things from the Dionysus crew. They were always honest, at least with me and blatantly direct.

"Good advice is a valuable thing. I wonder how you came by this good advice. Travelers present complications that ultimately diminish their chances," the oracle said.

"I try to be concise. My Book advised so," I agreed.

"Your Book? What am I permitted to know about this book you speak of?" she asked. She was intrigued yet humble, but I cannot be sure about her integrity. I'm going to assume she knows far more than she lets on.

"I was involved with a magic book that coached me on how to become like this," I offered, as I revealed my true appearance. "I suppose you are able to see beyond the magical disguise?"

"Travelers always present a nervous knot of complications, but you do not do so. I should be interested in knowing more about this book, but what are the two things you seek? Are they information? Travelers usually come looking for information," she volunteered.

"I am hoping to acquire two relics of significant power. I'm trying to find what are commonly called The Hand and The Eye of Hades," I stated frankly.

"Only one of those are within my sights. I cannot see the other," she declared after a long pause, with eyes closed and hands raised to her head as if she were listening or seeing somewhere in the distance. "The other is on a different plane: Gehenna 1 or Tarterus 1, I cannot see clearly. Both of these places seem important for some reason."

"May I know which is nearby? Is it The Hand or The Eye?" I asked sheepishly, suddenly realizing it was silly to ask remedial questions.

"Why does it matter? They are not in order, and getting one is a perfect success while getting none a perfect failure!" she adroitly responded.

"You are correct. I apologize. What is required to obtain the one nearby?" I asked.

"You must forfeit something of greater value, pecuniary measures applicable for non-enchantments only," she said.

"Understood. Please allow me some time to think," I said as politely as I possibly could.

"I have nothing but time," she admitted and immediately fell silent. Her image then disappeared.

I Teleport out, returning to Leipzig to think.

Chapter 13 : The Hand And The Eye

Another Surprise Or Two From Roxanne

Without any premeditated, predetermined destination in mind, and not having any clear idea of who to see or what to do, I find myself revisiting a special street in Ersa Calamy, disguised as a beggar, mingling in a crowd of pathetic derelicts, patiently trolling for a handout. I dart right into Roxy's blackened Tabernacle of The Hades Pantheon, an activity soon to become a habit. I'm always eager and excited to lay my contemptible, beady eyes upon Roxy and feast upon all her delicious physical assets. There I go again, talking like I know something, like I'm special. I am the lowest ranking dog. I am beneath the domestic bovine. The most dangerous person is one who has acquired a negligible amount of knowledge on a given subject, and with the fervor of the all-knowing erudite, inundates the public at large with an endless spew of utter balderdash. That's a valid description of me every time a fleeting image of Roxanne invades my consciousness, and you'll do yourself a favor to ignore me when I get started. Only two females have ever consistently taken my breath away and rendered me dumb, and both are, as I am made to understand, inside this very temple, right now. One is dead, but somehow continues to possess a powerful, spiritual hold over me that I admire and respect. The other is alive and soft and gorgeous, and she poses another kind of dominance upon me. Sometimes all I ever want is my mother, and maybe there is a lot of her in Roxy. Since I am physically prostate-free, I will manage to avoid embarrassing myself every time I come here. I cometh with a sense of privilege to simply gaze upon her.

"Come in, Ulmer. I did not expect you to be gone long."

Once again, that intimidating army of shiny obsidian rams follows me into Roxy's central chamber and blocks my exit. This is a dark and intensely atmospheric room, filling anyone but me with apprehension and trepidation. It is adorned with a huge stage and altar in the center, plenty big for dozens to stand about and witness a ritual or a ceremony take place. I hope Roxy doesn't use it to dig out my inner thoughts and fantasies. I don't know what I will do if that happens.

"Of course I intended to be back as soon as possible, and this time I did not visit my sisters. I came straight here," I said with a slight air of pride.

"I am glad. You are wise, Ulmer. Your baby sisters are good kids, they really are, but I worry about their choices and the lack of maturity to make them. They worship you, you must know that, Ulmer. They would follow you anywhere, to the bottom of the Abyss to tackle the Demogorgon if you ask them. My earlier judgement of them was perhaps a little harsh," she confided in earnest, and I realize I have to understand more about why she tells me these things. It's all so difficult and complicated for me to digest.

"Roxy, I want to share with you details concerning an ongoing project. I am hot onto the discovery and location of The Hand and The Eye of Hades. I think these artifacts could prove extremely beneficial, though I am weak to comprehend exactly how they would be best employed," I said proudly, but accidentally highlighting my naivety.

"Ulmer, are you contemplating employing these items yourself?" she asked calmly.

"Well, I had a thought. It seems to me that if we were to share one each - you take the hand so as not to mar your beautiful face, and I have the horrible eye, we could be forever bound together, and placed in position to become a major force throughout the world, you and I, together. I want to stand beside you, and the sisters would have no choice but to fall in line."

"Ulmer! I am deeply touched by your declaration and kind offer. I am moved by this suggestion, by your impartiality and frankness. But I really must wonder Ulmer, whether you have truly thought this through, whether perhaps you have misunderstood or forgotten who I am," Roxanne explained.

"Misunderstood, Roxy?" I nudged for more clarification, already feeling a little despondent, and even dispirited.

"Ulmer, you know I cannot place myself in contact with such relics. They were never intended for me. I am, by definition, the senior living prophet of Hades, the Unholy Grand Matriarch of the Dark Pantheon. I am completely human, unlike you and your siblings, and I know you know it. Those relics are meant for an entirely different purpose than what you propose. The Pantheon of Hades would not properly exist in this physical world if I were to go wild, my dear Ulmer. That would be a travesty for all of us and a boon to those sequestered Dionysus characters. I have chosen my distinguished position with integrity and care!" Roxanne explained with pronounced enthusiasm. Roxanne seemed to sparkle and glitter all over in a silvery twinkle as she spoke, and I was perfectly sucked in by her honorable declaration and pride.

"I see. I am sorry for my inexperience and shallowness," I apologized.

"I can help you locate and acquire these items if you wish, but they must not ever come here, and please do not tempt me directly with any such fanatical and demented notions ever again. I must strongly warn you and the girls about getting too close to these relics as well. Such items cannot allow you to further your agenda with poise and control," she advised.

"What do you suggest? Would I be better advised to forget them completely?" I asked.

"Having them change someone over toward us would be a stupendous victory. I would love to see that ignoramus Vortex get his due! But that would really mess things up," she suggested in jest. We both had a really good laugh over that one. "The Vortex could assume my position here and the Dionysus pantheon would be in terrible chaos. No, that would never do! How about that illusionist mentor of yours?"

"Raulston! Of course! I always lament his unwillingness to apply himself to any useful purpose. One of the two items is in The Tunnels of Blood. Lady Tansiméta will give it to me if I surrender something of higher value, and she's also able to provide clues to the existence of the other item," I explained, once again feeling much better. I'm completely invigorated working alongside this amazing woman. She is an inspirational leader and I am a miserable, worthless wretch in her presence. I try to get by with what I have.

"How did you become what you are? I know of precisely two pairs of The Hands and The Eyes. How did you learn of the Relics?" she quizzed.

"The Book! I have to get it back from Raulston and present it to The Oracle!" I exclaimed with confidence and determination. Now Roxanne can really see what a feeble twerp I am, but love and loyalty count for so much, right?

"Let's get busy learning more about your quest," Roxy suggested, and began invoking what I would soon learn is a Deity Commune, a powerful spell that allows her, or by extension another cleric of an established rank, to become knowledgable about anything provided sufficiently precise questions are asked. As I sit back to listen and watch, Roxanne would soon learn that The Oracle Tansiméta has The Hand, and that The Book is indeed a uniquely precious artifact, and that Tansiméta definitely hinted at her interest in it. Roxy then determined that The Eye is located on the Second Plane of Gehenna, close to but not exactly as Tansiméta had speculated. The Eye is in the ownership of, but not in the current use of a pair of influential but stupid Daerghodaemons called Boshnash the Skin Ripper and Filcher the Bone Crusher, both excellent names I thought! Roxy then disclosed that lesser daemons like these two meatheads would find themselves backed against the wall in her presence. They would be at a profound disadvantage against The Grand Matriarch of Hades, and so with that additional knowledge, I was pleased to witness Roxy enjoy her Devil Exaction immensely, a prodigiously powerful and dangerous spell that would light up the center stage in the room and present a most entertaining show. She wore a shiny black cape with a huge collar that covered her body and head completely, and still it looked so nice on her. That style fills me with anticipation.

Devil Exaction is an extraordinarily dangerous affair. The commitment as to how, whom, what and when embarks upon an epic tale, and once begun offers no guarantee of any lasting peace or reconciliation. Devil Exaction lets Roxy borrow Hades' extra dimensional Gate capabilities to name, summon and coerce a Devil, a Daemon or a Demon into some kind of service in exchange for an agreed upon counter favor or remuneration, something that you know right from the start will in most cases not ever work out as planned. The deepest humiliation this is likely to cause her named Daemon within its circle of influence will usually be considered a profound disrespect and must be avenged. But, having said all that, we mustn't underestimate who Roxanne is, what makes her special and why she will most easily hold herself above this danger.

"Give me Boshnash the Skin Ripper from Gehenna 2, a stupid piece of shit I hear! Make him and his cohort Filcher the Bone Crusher appear! I need to speak with them and make a deal. Boshnash and Filcher from The Second Level of Gehenna!" Roxy screamed toward the stage.

A huge whirlwind appeared on the stage, probably ten feet high and at least six feet across, and in a few moments the first hideously ugly Daergho appeared out of the whirlwind, cursing and hissing in the alignment tongue, the language of Neutral Evil. He had five arms, each with different lengths and three legs of different thicknesses, and his bulbous head spun around and around in a 360-degree turn upon his stout neck. What a sight! He must get so dizzy from all that spinning.

"Where is my Eye of Hades, you disgusting thief, Boshnash! Who do you think you are? Do you know who I am and what I will do if you don't immediately return my property?" demanded Roxanne, mostly screaming at the Daergho, and quite near the limit of her natural volume.

"I'm unsure! Let me bring up Filcher the Bone Crusher first! Perhaps he can advise better," screamed Boshnash, obviously in a fair bit of stress and discomfort. Roxanne must be administering a good amount of pressure from the sound of his panicked voice.

"Don't stall for time, Boshnash or I'll have one of your arms torn off and fed to your fucking boss for his lunch!" warned Roxanne at max-volume, in a punishingly loud baritone voice I had not ever imagined possible from her.

"Here he comes! Now there'll be trouble!" he predicted with a short, weak moment of confidence.

"What trouble would you dare make, you stupid idiot! Watch your mouth or I'll sew it shut for an eternity!" warned Roxy in that monstrous baritone.

Another great whirlwind produced another Daergho, this one turning into the predicted Filcher the Bone Crusher. He appeared badly disoriented and dizzy, head spinning round and round, barely able to collect himself as Roxy accosted him.

"Filcher, Boshnash tells me you stole my Eye of Hades. When are you thinking to give it back, you miserable thieving pile of demon shit?" Roxy started off strong.

"What? No no, wait! That's not right! I didn't steal it! He did! It wasn't me, Roxanne, it was him, Boshnash!" protested Filcher in a panic, fingering his own cohort like a baby.

At that moment, Roxanne whisked off the black cape, much to my satisfaction, exposing very nearly all of her feminine beauty. She was wound up tight with potential against these halfwitted Daerghodaemons. This enlisted an additional surge, another wave of influence that was unexpected by all of us. It seemed to assist with her remarkable control of the situation, releasing another level of power. I just sat back smiling, gratified with the confidence this cleric exudes.

"Roxanne, no please! Please don't! We promise we'll bring it up. Just let Boshnash go down and get it, as long as you promise two things. You must promise to leave us alone and promise not to tell any of our superiors about this incident. Promise, promise and we'll give you your thing!" cried Filcher and Boshnash in tandem, both in extreme despair.

"OK, I'll be waiting, and I'm not letting Filcher go until you get back with my item, Boshnash. Don't even think to mess this up! Ulmer, get up on that stage, and I'll get Boshnash to hand it to you. You must Teleport out of here immediately. That abomination cannot remain in my temple. Understand?" shouted Roxy at me and the Daerghos at once.

"I understand," I said loudly as I jumped up onto the stage beside Filcher. What a rush to be standing right next to this hideous creature from a nether plane like this, its existence never known to me before today. When Boshnash appeared with a small, ornate box with a handle and key, Roxy had one more thing to say before I Teleported to my favorite hotel in Fered Soudron.

"Filcher, Boshnash, you two nipple heads better not be deceiving me, I'll say it just once. If you do, the deal is off! And then you'll wish you were forever fucking dead whenever you think of me! You shall never know peace!" she warned in earnest, just as Boshnash handed me the box. I was out. What a woman! These clerics have some skills! My goodness, I had no idea this is what my mother might have become if Kangas hadn't gotten so messed up.

Tansiméta Produces The Hand

Another Deity Commune spell next day is accompanied by a string of Font Scries. The spell lets us peer into Roxanne's Scrying Basin and see whatever and wherever we wish to see. Working the Commune and the Scries allows Roxy to pinpoint Raulston's new clandestine accommodation in Milan, and I can easily judge from the predictable layout of his extensive library where The Book is likely stored.

"We have to be careful, here Ulmer. He might see," Roxy warned.

"He likes to go out in the evenings," I remembered, and during times of his absence, we are able to Font Scry effectively across his huge and ever-growing library. It is quite fun, especially for me, to review the titles I was intimately familiar with, and others I have never seen.

"If we can pinpoint the precise location of The Book, I can Teleport in, grab it and Teleport back within a minute. The concern is I have never been to Milan so I must make a practice trip first to make sure there is no mistake," I said, and with that decent plan in process, we are able to accomplish the task the very next day. Fred G. and Mr. Learus are not often home, spending a considerable amount of time adventuring with the young Dionysus cleric Karim and Kadrah the Druid, and a double-check with a Deity Commune reveals the desired news. All the illusionists are out.

I'm living modestly, spread evenly between Roxy's temple and my favorite Fered Soudron hotel. I wanted to find something suitable right here in central Ersa Calamy, but nobody would ever suspect a thing in Fered Soudron, and as a result keeping a little distance works out to my advantage.

After two days of rest and study, The Book and I Teleport all the way up to the Oracle Tansiméta, to The distant Tunnels of Blood, probably some 55 or 60 days from here, measured by the most conventional mode of transport.

"Feel free to ask for what I may grant you ?" instructed the middle-aged female figure, standing on the platform in her bright ceremonial costume, all exactly as before. Her arms are fully extended with hands at waist height, but this time her palms are face up and held out straight toward me. This gesture was noticeably different, and I may hope I am placed on a higher level.

"Lady Tansiméta, I have come to follow up on our previous discussion. I would like to acquire The Hand of Hades," I proudly stated.

"Travelers so often present their own challenges and complications," stated the Oracle plainly.

"Yes, I worried about that, dear Lady. I made sure to bring along something that I believe will prove a satisfactory trade for The Hand of Hades. I have brought The Book we discussed, The Book that made me what I am," I explained as I held it out.

The Oracle looked down, studying the tome with eyes closed with one hand raised to her temple. "This is a very unique artifact and constitutes a satisfactory trade for the item you seek," she declared, and in the next moment a small ornamental box with a handle and key, very similar to the other one, appeared on one of the pedestals outside the pool area. This similar appearance does instill a good amount of confidence in the authenticity of both items. And The Book disappeared.

"Thank you, Dear Lady Tansiméta," I stated, and teleported clear across the enormous journey back to Fered Soudron in an instant. What a rush! It's good to be me!

Baby Step Sisters Layla and Lorelei

"Ulmer, dear brother, why do you play with us like this? Don't you understand how we feel? We are family. We love you. We live for you. We belong together. Please don't disappear again without keeping us informed. It isn't fair! We know you spend more time with Roxanne. What does she do that we don't? Huh? What does she have that we don't?" protested both Layla and Lorelei in perfect stereo, one on one side with her tongue in my ear, the other licking and tickling my tailbone like before, right around where my prostate used to be. They know I like those things but oddly I can never guess which one is which at the moment. I actually like coming here. Things are really not so bad.

"I've been busy. Roxanne has only the kindest words for you, don't panic! It's all about us!" I insisted, but looks of frustration and disbelief still pervade their inquisitive attitude.

"Ulmer, we know you've been philandering around us. We're watching you all the time. You can't hide from us, you know," they warned as they unveiled their previously hidden Scrying Font.

"That's a handy tool. I only just learned about those things a couple of days ago. Roxy and I were watching some POI," I said cheerfully, not trying to roll my eyes too obviously. "I guess now that I know, I'll be able to see you when you're watching me, isn't that right?"

That comment was met with silence and a pair of disgruntled stares. My baby step sisters are so cute, but also so easily predictable. I'm sorry to say this, but these girls are stuck beneath me. I hope that changes just a little, and their ambition does lead me to worry about what they might do to get their way, but at this moment I judge them in some need of remedial care. Attention is needed here, and I can be well advised to give some consideration to a range of tasks I should lay before them. Roxy hinted at that. Shit slides downhill, but it doesn't have to be toxic. I'm going to put these mutts to work.

Roxy's Solitary Gehenna Excursion

"Ulmer, I'm going to Gehenna to visit Filcher and Boshnash. They miraculously held up their end of our bargain, and as long as I hold up ours, we'll be fine. If however, I go down there and offer them a reward for their services, they will be forever bound to us, forever our ally in Gehenna 2. You just never know what use these two meatheads might be," explained Roxanne in a particularly good mood.

She's been scheming lately, especially since the topic of relics was burned into her consciousness.

"I should be proud to accompany you, dear Roxanne," I proposed. I would be proud to go anywhere with Roxy, to be seen with her, to be tied into all her hobbies and activities. Just let the rumor mill go wild. Let it connect her to me in any imaginable way, because it cannot possibly do me any harm. It is good publicity. I am sick.

"Later, we will, as long as this turns out no less than expected. I'll Astral Travel by myself this journey. I'll be fine leaving from here," she confided. "If possible, come check on me in exactly three days. I'll be sitting right here, in front of my prayer altar, and expect to return within the following hour. It is best that you stay until I return, but if all goes as planned, I'll be back here exactly on time."

And with that we parted ways with her Astral adventure commencing, and my return to Fered Soudron, sitting on the ordinary hotel bed, a single width mattress on a squeaky cot, just me, my spell books, and my two priceless artifacts.

Good-bye Raulston Dear Mentor

Watching Raulston's activities for a while, I get some sense for Milan on one of its sunniest days. It's a messy, disorganized and unclean kind of urban conundrum. What would make Raulston want to ditch Fered Soudron and come here is not apparent, but a little research deeper into the question reveals why Milan exhibits a number of important features. The Assassins Guild, The Thieves Guild and The Monks Guild are all located here. The young Dionysus cleric Karim is proving to be a steady acquaintance to the illusionists and his recent establishment in Milan is no accident. A Dionysus cleric can do much here. Kadrah and The Druid Stronghold are also nearby, immediately across the river bridge, though a generally overall, dark and sooty atmosphere is evident in much of the city. My understanding is that Kadrah is closely aligned with The Assassins as well. I wonder what would be the logic behind such an alliance. There has to be something because Kadrah does not strike me as the sort to act without first conducting a careful analysis of whatever he sets his mind into. Could he be dual-classed as well?

Milan southwest is especially bad. Here the concentration of illicit activity easily overshadows the worst precinct of my former Kangas. I witness homeless people and neglected, diseased livestock just ignored as they pass away alone in the streets. Carcasses and piles of rubbish lie about everywhere and "Disease Control Specialists Urgently Wanted" are to be important job postings by city officials scrambling to find patchy solutions, far too few and much too late.

On the midday before I am bound attendance to my beloved Roxanne, I find Raulston home alone and make myself known to him.

"Damn you Ulmer! I'm sick of you and your bullshit! Why do I have you to put up with? Why can't you be normal and polite like Fred G. Gearbox?" he started off at me.

"Dear mentor, don't be angry. I've only ever had our best intentions at heart. I have brought something that should be of great interest to us," I said calmly, trying to display an uplifting air of anticipation.

As I place the two boxes neatly side by side upon his desk, I realize that he has probably not noticed the missing book. That can only mean exactly as I had for years prognosticated, that he has never held much stock in anything outside his steadfast allegiance to Team Dionysus.

"What are these, then?" he asked gruffly. "And why don't you take off that stupid disguise? It's dumb."

I produced the two keys required to unlock the boxes. He grabbed them in anger and haste. It felt as though the reckoning of a prophecy was at hand, all set to be experienced, right here and now. As he turned the keys, the lids popped gently open, revealing the contents. Both items, as ominous as they were to witness up close, were neatly laid in plush, red velvet moulds.

Raulston was transfixed with interest, just staring in wonder. He used True Sight and Identify spells to try and learn more, mostly to no avail. He then made an effort to remove The Hand from its box, thinking that in the process of the Identify spell, a physical connection would provide more results. Raulston began to smile brightly, as though he were gradually becoming absorbed in some hallucinatory euphoria, and with The Hand clutched between his own, its fingers pointed up, a large, shining blade, probably mithril, suddenly appeared. Raulston was overtaken with an overwhelming urge to bludgeon himself in the right eye with the blade. He began to howl in anger and scream in pain as he continued to gouge himself, over and over again, completely submerged by an inexplicable urge to torture and deface himself, ever so violently and terribly. He screamed and sobbed in non-stop terror as blood poured out of his head, all over his desk, his books and everywhere. He was completely consumed by the horror of his actions, and at once appeared to enjoy it all in some bizarre way, and would therefore not stop.

By now, he had fully carved his right eye out of his head and from his face. It fell onto his desk with a disgusting splat. Its eyeball continued to look around and around, and the countless nerve endings were moving aimlessly about, like a dying fish on a chef's dinner plate. The handy carving work left a gaping, bloody, black hole in his head where his right eye used to be. This development was not at all helpful to his charisma, but rather than fading out of consciousness as might be expected, Raulston removed The Eye from the box and held it up to the right side of his head. In horror and disbelief, I could witness The Eye enter his head and attach itself to him, attach itself to his brain and nervous system, becoming part of him as though it had always been there. Raulston continued to scream in excruciating pain, even as I removed all my disguises and cloth coverings, allowing him at last to see who and what I am, what I have become. I begin to laugh, and it isn't that I recognize any comedy here, but that all the insanity of this is beginning to rub off on me in another way. As I lose cognitive images and memories of Paulina and Roxy, I am profoundly reminded of myself, of who I am and what I have become. Oh, my dear sweet Layla and Lorelei! Are you watching now? Because now is the time to be watching, if ever there were a time! You can see me for real now!

The Eye was a fair bit too large for Raulston's head, and collectively he and it, or they decided to make some physical adjustments to accommodate the oversized organ. Raulston affected this by manually carving out a larger eye cavity in his skull. He did all this himself, holding The Hand between his own two, and manipulating the utensils as best he could. It was not a scientific process. Bits of his brain began oozing out of his head, and this could not count as a positive in the longer term. Recognizing the deficiency, he bent over and sucked his former eye and bits of the brain tissue into his mouth and began to chew. He swallowed down his former eye like a freshwater oyster. Raulston would never pass his practical examinations in medical school, but he somehow did manage to complete the required adjustments. His whole head changed shape once The Eye had seated itself to its satisfaction, and his skull took on this horrible, disfigured look that would horrify everyone. The Eye began to glow brightly, and Raulston smiled for a moment, experiencing a respite from all the terror and the unbearable pain.

For a short time, it seemed things were settling. Raulston was beginning to see through The Eye, and he started to feel huge. His hair was turning a brittle, crackly white. Some of his teeth fell out of his mouth, and he nearly choked on one that went down the wrong way. He fell to the floor, coughing uncontrollably for a while until the problem was corrected, and I had another good laugh, remembering a similar experience not very long ago, back in Cirsalsomere.

All was under control at last, and he genuinely appeared content and relaxed, enjoying a well-deserved rest. But then The Hand, which had fallen onto the floor, crawled over like a spider with missing legs and poked at him. This sent him up into a new terror, a chaotic frenzy he was ill-prepared for. He was completely beside himself. The Hand was beckoning itself to him. Raulston panicked again and again, this time running about room to room totally crazed, opening and closing desk drawers and closet doors looking for something. He ran into the next room; he came running back, opening and slamming shut doors. Back to the next room he went again, reappearing with what looked to be a rusty old bone saw, the kind a butcher uses to remove large slabs from the surrounding bone. Raulston put his left forearm down on the desk flat and tout de suite began to saw his helpless left hand clear off, right at the wrist. The initial anguish was quite pronounced, but overall it was a relatively cleanly administered operation, at least compared to the previous one, and I saw how Raulston was now well beyond any discomfort associated with The Eye. It was as though he were now enjoying, even savoring every subsequent moment. When the unnecessary body parts were removed, The Hand could easily be fitted into place. This must be such a relief. Large, hideous protrusions began growing all over his face, neck and head, and I had a vision of my poor, sweet brother Usain, but this was even worse. This was just horrifying, but neither of us cared any longer. The transformation was moving into its final stage of completion. Raulston was now a servant of Hades, and bound to obey me as well, a complete and total role reversal. This instant, however, he Teleported out, and so I did the same. I flopped myself into a comfortable black leather sofa at Roxanne's, looking around at all the luxury, and feeling quite content with all my accomplishments these past few heady days. It is good to be me.

Chapter 14 : The Calm Before The Storm

"Ulmer, Lori and I are not happy. You don't love me and you don't love her. You never consider us. You spend all your time lazing around in that bitch Roxanne's bed and don't even come home to say 'Hello' to your own baby, sweet sisters. We're over here crying. We cry day and night! Roxanne probably treats you like some big shot emperor or something, doesn't she, Ulmer? She makes you feel so fucking important. I'll bet Roxy licks you so clean every time, you can't say shit. She has you totally thrashed. You have no idea how she uses you for whatever evil purpose suits her fancy. She shellacs every bone on you - you're as shiny as a jewel, aren't you, Ulmer?" on and on Layla ranted, consumed in her whiny tirade from the moment I showed up. It was several weeks later than they had expected. I guess I had it coming.

"Girls, girls! Really, it isn't true. You are totally over-reacting! I've been busy. You two are most important to me! Honestly! By the way, isn't it a bad omen to run down your mentor that way?" I objected, pretending concern but displaying an obvious smirk, fighting hard to hold in my laughter.

This reaction is guaranteed to invite serious trouble. All the same, these two mutts are totally endearing, I have to admit, and adorable despite all the whining and exposed boney body parts. In general, I remonstrate against baby talk and lodge a formal protest at being used as a floor mop, and to make progress, the time has come to take this relationship to another level. I'll put these air heads to work; let them experience my life on my account.

"We've prepared a nice little bed and study room for you. You have a home, Ulmer. It's a real home here with us," Lorelei boasted with enthusiasm, and then both escort me into the little dungeon they obsessed over. Amazing to me is how they put so much emphasis into the bed, plush and girly and expansive as it is, and so little into my study. They have limited understanding of what I do so corrective education commences today. Alter Reality and Permanent Illusion affect the necessary adjustments, much to their surprise, and although the girls complain at my general lack of concept concerning interior design, they are forced to concede my need for more space, a lot more.

"Girls, come here. I have a mission for you. I have chronic difficulties with my mentor. He is not the same person and I struggle unnecessarily. I need to get in front of this," I said.

My sisters are exuberant, an agreeable convenience I may freely exploit. They sympathize with the mentor problem. While down-playing the significance of the two evil artifacts employed in the ordeal, I inform them in general terms about what transpired. We brainstorm ways of bringing their Deity Commune, Divine Prediction, Scrying Font and other powers to the table to track Raulston's location and ongoing activities. It isn't an easy process because he is erratic and unfocused. The activity requires diligent concentration and continuous verification. But two clerics are infinitely better than one and the girls are pleased to be of use. Lori wonders perhaps a Continuous Darkness inside the Font room might reduce the chance of being detected. While not exactly an expert on cleric duties, I will remark about the resourcefulness. The girls show incredible brilliance when facilitated with appropriate conditions!

The next project has me making regular watches of Raulston's study in Milan, and with the other illusionists generally away and out of the way, I am granted license to Teleport in, grab hold of an item or two that has long been of interest, and pilfer it. One of those is the RILF! Oh, how wonderful it is to own this beautiful device again! Raulston won't be needing it anymore, I shouldn't think. Within a few months, I hope to accumulate and curate an impressive library and collection of devices, though still a heavily abridged one - we cannot have Fred G. suspicious. This arcane material connects and binds Raulston and I, and confiscating it hopefully does not arouse panic in anyone outside our circle. Anyway, Raulston owns a enormous amount of interesting stuff, and the other guys will probably not miss those particular few items I want.

My little residence at Layla and Lori's begins to work out well. The girls are more cheerful and don't complain even when I slip out for Roxy's regular nightly bone lickings. I take every precaution to remain anonymous and keep myself, my activities and my possessions well hidden. Shaman Learus has now also relocated to Ersa Calamy, taking up residence at the Dionysus Monestario. In addition to adventuring alone, Fred G. spends a lot of time in Leipzig and also collaborates with the Druids. Everything is set, and so far, nobody is aware of, or has any reason to suspect, my involvement in Raulston's behavior. It just appears to be his own madness and lack of self-control, and that is precisely what sets us apart! I am not mad, at least not yet.

Raulston is now wallowing in what I would call his gestation period. He spends a lot of time in profound misery, sadness and despair. He seems to be met with nothing but difficulties wherever he goes, and there comes a day in late 688 when his depression overtakes his ability to function. My understanding is that in this circumstance, The Hand and The Eye will seek the death of their host and move on to another as quickly as possible. The Hand will even perpetrate the suicide if a suitable candidate is nearby. Some time before that moment would obviously be an ideal time to intervene and lend a hand. A respite from terror instills a boost of confidence, great for getting at least another year out of Raulston, hopefully more.

Raulston makes trips to Cirsalsomere. There are indeed some inexplicable connections between us, though I am sure Raulston's fond memories of our early days together somehow screw with his powerful subconscious. Together they influence his actions to some extent.

In his heightened state of awareness, he has discovered another something of particular interest to me. He has located an ancient burial site, a massive, walled cemetery near the extreme west coast, a place I will call the Peninsula of Hate, lying directly west of Cirsalsomere.

Digging deeper, I discover twenty separate tombs, each with identical catacombs filled with mummies. Why it is there is far from clear, but the condition is incredibly derelict and must be older than common written history. This will be something to investigate as soon as I can make time.

I Teleport to him one day, taking great care not to startle him into reacting badly and doing something stupid. I have to ease into this with care, hoping to catch him in a mellow state of sorrow. If I do this right, establishing this first contact will hopefully bring him significant relief.

"Raulston!" I literally whispered, hiding behind one of the burial mounds built over each tomb.

He reeled about this way and that. "What? Who's there?" he inquired several times, obviously agitated but not too badly startled. "Who's there?"

"Ulmer, it's me, Ulmer," I whispered, not knowing how he would respond. He could be anywhere between murderously angry to enormously relieved to see me. It has been over a year and he might justify any reaction. What I can say is that he will at some point need to acknowledge my superiority and get on board. Role reversal is at hand, and it needs to happen because I have work to delegate.

"Raulston! Kangas has to slide into complete ruin. Your new toys allow you to transform low level humans and other simple creatures into undead. All we need is a few hundred wights loose in Kangas without warning, and within a year or two, the entire remnant of twelve thousand weakened survivors will be overrun," I explained. "There can be no survivors if you lock the city down, raise the drawbridges and lower the portcullises. Don't throw away any keys. Hang them down in the city armory bunker, on the wall and label them for reference. That location is mostly secret to the general population."

"Yeah, Yeah," he chuckled "What an idea. I can do that. Yeah, OK," he agreed.

"When you're done Kangas - that's the easy job - you can start making trouble for Leipzig. That should be at least a year from now. Go slow at first. Don't get caught. Just do little things there, not anything horrible like making undead. Let's carefully monitor how they react. Then lay off for a while. See if you can get life miserable for that jerk-off, Joey. I guess they call him Kalaringus Tell. I call him Jerk-off Joey. He's extremely powerful so be careful," I warned, and I didn't see Raulston again for another year, at least not in person.

The girls continued to watch him and record his activities through Layla's Font. They did this several times a week. He was busy in Kangas for all of 689 and into 690, and his time there was like a vacation.

As we watch Raulston making his transition toward Leipzig, I sense his invigorated evil spirit develop. He is no longer desperate and seems to get along with an improved sense of purpose. This can also have the undesirable outcome of becoming overly confident and careless, but right now he is in positive territory.

I look away, occupied with other things, and by mid 690, understand that Kangas has veritably fallen into complete annihilation. Undead are so useful, helping us by facilitating all this terror. No obligation to remunerate or feed makes them better than slaves.

The coming year and a half gets Raulston focused on Leipzig while I steer my concentration toward the Peninsula of Hate. I set myself up in the private house of the former mayor and feel mighty good about my skill at ordering undead around like servants. The House of Lilly is completely derelict, and anyway memories of that place are just too sad and I choose to keep away. I can toggle between Kangas and Ersa Calamy now, and for much of the foreseeable future, I'll split myself between both locations. There is so much to do, and placing myself at the helm of Kangas seems ironically appropriate after all these years. Reacquainting myself with dogs is fun, though none are left who remember me, and the others for some reason growl more than they used to. I must allow for their severe but understandable anxiety and mistrust. Kangas is no longer populated by humans. I am no longer human, and the dogs are wise to take extra care.

A detailed map of the Peninsula dungeon configuration is a starting point, and over the next eight months, I focus on affecting considerable changes to each of the tombs, modifications that address my unique purposes. Details have to suit my circumstances, for I am now drifting downhill, trapped in my own miserable quicksand. These tombs facilitate the conversion of selected followers from Kangas and a few ancient mummies into liches. How this works needs to remain proprietary for now, and there are several possibilities to experiment with, but also one major weakness. I might need Raulston for help, that is, the new-and-improved Raulston, the one answerable to Yours Truly.

Chapter 15 : Early 692

The Year-End Imagined

Someone somewhere is going to present 692 as the most commodious year in the history of the West, and I'm going to be nominated Man of the Year. I'll be found on the cover of all the yearbooks. I'm going to be on the front page of year-end papers and journals. I'll be featured in almanacs as the P.O.I. of 692. Curiously, no one has the slightest idea of what I actually look like, so the rumor mill will be loads of fun. Elementary schools will have drawing and painting contests, and winners in each institution will be featured and celebrated at public show-and-tells. Parents will gush with enthusiasm. I can help every kid get their fifteen minutes of fame. In Milan, the prettiest little 6-year-old girl anyone ever saw anywhere named Ninmeşaora, drew a caricature of "Ulmaetor the Great". That submission earned the little charmer a generous scholarship to a named art school. In a courageous public announcement that further boosted widespread interest, the little mouthpiece respectfully declined the prestigious offer, citing a firm intention to one day commit herself to becoming a spiritual person of prayer. Oh, great! Another one! Then there was young Burk, a 7-year-old boy from an affluent Milanese business family, said he wanted to personally present a home-made Get-Well Card, that apparently he'd heard I had caught a cold. Just what I need! A fucking Get-Well Card!

"A Man, you say? Really? A Man? That is something. Oh no, I don't think Ulmaetor is a man!" Ninmeşaora publicly stated. Well, what d'ya know about that?

Layla and Lori have been scripted to tell exhaustive stories about how I had made precisely two appearances at their Temple, and that both were so random and unexpected, and that I must have been so covered up that they could not possibly have identified me then, nor could they provide any worthwhile clues regarding appearances now. They did mention that they thought my voice to be rather gruff. What the girls will do, and it's something into which the public will be most gratified to acquiesce, is take a guess at what I might have looked like. This is reportage of the highest journalistic integrity, and that is what sells newspapers, much like estimating death tolls after natural disasters.

Roxanne has a strict policy of not discussing anything about anyone patronizing her premises, and while the news industry derides her as being boring, uncaring and aloof, and that she is most certainly not a team player, she somehow manages to eek out a satisfactory amount of free publicity anyway. Who would have ever imagined such a thing - as though she gives a shit what anyone says.

But seriously, we are getting ahead of ourselves. The story of 692 hasn't been told yet, because 692 hasn't happened yet, and heads will spin right off our necks like a Daerghodaemon with a migraine once we appreciate all there is to absorb. From that moment onward, we will be involved in a dramatically different tale, and the camp we're cheering for when we revisit this auspicious time will need an urgent reassessment.

Surprise Apollo and Aphrodite Establishments

More than a few times have I allowed a bad mood to impede my thinking. This is a habit that I must unlearn. More than a few times do I feel myself sinking into the darkest chasm, and allow myself to go there. There are still moments when I think about my parents and my brother, moments that make me tremendously angry. I cannot ever seem to grow beyond nurturing these wicked thoughts. They were benign, invasive irritations at first, nothing more, but they gradually started creeping about everywhere inside me, ultimately dominating my consciousness. That has not been a recent phenomenon as you know. I vividly remember the Darkness that overpowered me even when I was a boy. The Dark is my only real motivation now, I must acknowledge, and I suppose you must have long ago guessed it. The Dark is my salvation.

Raulston moved to Milan to have better access to others relevant to him within the Dionysus realm. But ever since I invaded his privacy and set him on a path geared toward my objectives, other things have manifested in Milan that nobody saw coming. I'm sure it's just coincidence. The Pantheons of Apollo and Aphrodite, heretofore considered irrelevant and inept, suddenly established themselves there. The Patriarch of Apollo is St. Bodan, a dude obviously poised to win the Activist of the Year award. He will turn Milan upside down. The Aphrodite Matriarch is Genoivieve, and while she is at this point a mere child, she is fully endowed with the goods. They will soon present enough leverage to rival the girls in my circle, perhaps even challenge me, and I foresee another headache coming. Milan will immediately feel this change, and it will become a major issue for Raulston and The Three Guilds. They'll hate it. Why, you may wonder, when we are made to understand that the Neutral Alliance isn't evil? There is a long list of plausible hypotheses, but one that I can state with certainty is that the general public is going to swarm around these two newcomers like maggots on a dead rat. The balance has shifted and civil strife is on the horizon. This is Milan and we expect it to be ugly.

One Dionysus Member Condemned

Under the auspices of The Vortex, The Neutral Alliance has begun exercising its will. We have Raulston and Fred G. tearing around like berserkers, driving everyone nuts. The problem is they aren't berserk. We see Kadrah the Druid, Shaman Learus and the young Dionysus acolyte Karim adventuring together, which I suppose is fine, but the greater concern is the deepening ties the illusionists and The Druids appear to be forging with thieves, monks and assassins. The Guilds are powerful. The Neutral Alliance is spreading itself broadly across an expansive field of influence, and a few things begin to happen that even the most gifted augur could not have seen coming for all the bribes in the World.

The Grand Master of the Thieves Guild, based in Milan, has taken a particular interest in Raulston's less than subtle activities. The Grandmaster, as he shall be called, in part because his name is never made public, has noticed that Raulston's study is precariously unprotected. Thieves are in the business of thieving, and it doesn't take long before The Grandmaster and a handful of skilled henchmen begin helping themselves to Raulston's magnificent hoard.

Two significant miscalculations present some noteworthy conditions. Firstly, The Thieves Guild Members incorrectly assumed that removing Raulston's hoard one item at a time would not set off any red flags. We can understand from this that thieves are not deeply educated in what illusionists can and probably will do in retaliation. This is simply not the same set of conditions nor the same strategy as when I was doing exactly that: looting one item at a time. Secondly, and probably more importantly, is realizing that Fred G. Gearbox's methods are malicious over-reactions, and rather than confronting those who would, under normal circumstances be his allies, Fred G. Gearbox sets up a trap that perpetrates the single-handed assassination of The Grandmaster. They have never seen eye to eye, and I see how this is the next obvious thing to happen.

For all the things we may have come to understand about Fred G., one important fact cannot be debated: he is powerful and dangerous. He possesses confidence, great skill and determination and utilizes his powers in ways that cause even Raulston to do a double-take. Inside Raulston's, Fred sets up Permanent Illusions, Phantasmal Forces and Phantasmal Killers to instill disorientation, confusion and terror in the thieves. But he does not depend on these powerful things to complete the task. Fred merely seeks to skew the advantage temporarily by affecting sudden and ongoing visual changes designed to confuse. Upon entering the premises, The Grandmaster is point-blank bombarded with an illusionary Cone of Cold, a powerful and explosive Phantasmal Force, and one that damages nothing else inside. Fred then depends on his own stealth and secrecy to destroy The Grandmaster at his own game. He uses illusionary disguises and a surprise dagger attack, coming in from behind, going straight for the throat. Badly overwhelmed, The Grandmaster reels about, attempting to retreat and disappear into the shadows, except that this is when the Programmed Illusion kicks in by altering the scene, confusing the thief yet again. The entire room flashes and shifts about, and nothing appears as it was. This gives the thief another problem to overcome, and the delay is costly. Fred G. completes his mission by employing a point-blank illusionary lightning bolt. It was such a close-range attack that a real one would have caused significant injury to himself upon release, but of course the illusion injures only those who believe it to be true.

And so ended the reign of The Grandmaster of Thieves, if I may call it a reign at all. He wasn't much liked and henchmen were nowhere left to be seen. Everyone goes on to assume Raulston was the mastermind behind the assassination here today, and Guild Members rejoice at the opportunity to vie amongst one another for the top job. No effort was made to assist or rescue The Grandmaster. There was no honor left to speak of there. Thieves have no honor, but thankfully illusionists do. Four especially precious magical daggers are added to Fred's arsenal. Fred then determines the body to be good swine feed, noting that pigs will happily eat anything and everything.

Another Dionysus Member Condemned

Raulston was not the perp like everyone assumed. It was a beautifully master-minded undertaking, orchestrated by the

Gearbox himself, and you would be forgiven for thinking he was done and satisfied. He was not. Greed and an insatiable lust for power are elements that drag the G deep down toward the Dark, and not too far from me, though I must clearly state that my personal objectives and motivations are not as ignoble. I knew it and he knew it, way back on our very first meeting in Fered Soudron years ago. Who can remember when that even was?!

Raulston got consumed in his activities to the point of raising the ire of all the known pantheons. He even tried to take on Kalaringus Tell, surely another poor judgement call. The balance has been upset. Did Gearbox get singled out for any involvement? I don't think so. Did I get the accolades and publicity I was predicting? It was wishful thinking. Fame is not always a good thing.

Long before I could settle myself into a project worth applying myself to, Gearbox acted yet again. He collected his buddy Kadrah the Great Druid. He rounded up the young Dionysus cleric Karim. He got the nod from but not the active involvement of Shaman Learus, Raulston's third apprentice living in Ersa Calamy. Gearbox even solicited full support from the fledgling Apollo group, the young but well established Ranger Marshall Kesselring, coming all the way from Leipzig.

They set it up very well, presiding over the most important and most public assassination in recent memory. Gearbox supervised and superintended a mission to acquire the two things that he wanted: Raulston's position and all his possessions, including some of what was filched by the Guild. We learned something about Kadrah from this as well. We surmise the nature of his involvement with a certain other Guild in Milan. I have long wondered about that myself, but let's understand that Druids care more about the maintenance of neutrality than the assumed indifference to other alignments.

The Hand and The Eye were an abnormally gargantuan concern. The esteemed team of assassins wisely recognized the danger and took several necessary precautions. Gearbox devised an acceptable solution, employing an Alter Reality to send the Relics into the care of The Oracle Tansiméta. He no doubt hopes to put those miserable abominations out of sight and out of mind forever. The guy's wisdom never disappoints. All this I learn from my dearest baby step sisters Layla and Lorelei, engrossed in their craft, driven by a determination to be indispensable. They monitored Raulston with flawless precision.

It will take some time to fully comprehend all of what has transpired. I think a nice holiday might be in order. Kangas has a top hotel but the amenities have declined in recent years. My former mentor Raulston is gone; that much is certain. I am ultimately to blame for that. Gearbox has suddenly garnered a position of respect, a point I would prefer to publicly refute, but I'm not sure it's all bad. Have they simply toppled and deposed a total madman with another one? Gearbox has also inadvertently shown a color I did not expect. Despite appearances, he is firmly entrenched in the Dionysus temperament. This is disappointing. Vespertine just shrugs his shoulders at what Fred has done and days, "Aw Poor Raulston! I liked the old fart. I suppose we'll miss'im!"

I feel the bizarre attraction of The Dionysus school of thought for a brief moment and it fizzles away. I had too many expectations concerning both Raulston and The G. I'll have to alter strategy. The Relics of Hades are gone, but not so far gone that I cannot feel them. I alone understand both of what they are and where they are, and having them safely locked away from anyone's grasp is my advantage. I have time to consider my long term plans as well as next moves. The Lady Oracle Tansiméta and I are old friends. We have an understanding and we belong together. Neither of us are going anywhere, and she can feel free to hold on to them until I get beyond this delusional, psychoneurotic state I must be in.

Chapter 16 : Late 692

"Layla, who was Lorelei's father and why did Mother die in childbirth?" I asked point blank, immediately after Teleporting in. I popped in without warning, giving the girls no chance to collect their thoughts. I learned the power of that cruel strategy watching Fred G. I witnessed first hand how and why The Grandmaster could never have anticipated outright demise by his own trade.

"Ohhh, hello dear brother!" Layla cheerfully responded, wearing a bright smile, but also sounding nervous. "Lorelei and I had different fathers, we know that. But we never learned who they were. Confidentiality was harshly enforced, and so we were forbidden to Commune anything concerning it when we got established," Layla was able to explain. She seemed content to divulge that much, probably substantiating its truth.

"Someone from the Greenbone elite maybe?" I wondered, mostly doubting the thought. I am in no hurry to let on too much, either.

"We can't imagine it. We know it's from below; just look at us - bones sticking out everywhere! Who it was and from where exactly, however remains a mystery," she confided.

"I'm going to get to the bottom of this. My bones are bare as well. I think we owe Mother at least that much respect," I said in a determined voice.

"Ulmer, don't dig too deep into these things, please Ulmer, dear brother," Lorelei interjected, worried about my impatient behavior. There is a carelessness in my personality that makes family members nervous. My sisters are not simply pointing out my irrationality. They are afraid.

"I don't want anyone upset and disappointed," she added in resignation. "Things will come out we might prefer not to know."

Now the girls have grabbed my attention, and I surely have theirs. Why would Lori say that if there weren't something menacing and juicy hidden away in there, knowledge that big brother isn't privy to? The sisters may not even possess all the details, but are masterful at differentiating good from bad and occasionally even right from wrong, and this is sounding like something more than just another typical tale of evil intent at work.

"I'm out of here," I concluded, and immediately disappeared. This project has been on my mind for years, and the time to act has come.

One Resurrection in Hades

"Roxanne, I'm ready. Let's do this," I said all excited the moment I teleported in. The obsidian rams were surprised but marshaled into their defensive formation in a flash. I love my new style.

"Ready for what, Ulmer?" she asked innocently.

"The Resurrection of Paulina Lilly. Let's do it," I urged, feeling brave and ambitious. I like pretending to be prepared.

"It's been over two years! I really thought you'd written it off, long forgotten about it. You know, once these things are set in motion, they cannot be stopped. Some things cannot be undone. Many terrible things are best left alone. Look closely at what happened to your Hand and Eye of Hades project. It was a fucking fiasco, but it was not your fault. You were its pawn, same as your poor, innocent mentor. The outcomes are beyond our control," warned Roxy, pretending to sound only like she wasn't in the mood to exert herself. She did very much savor her words nonetheless, and I shouldn't be astonished that she's been tracking my activities as closely as the sisters down the street. Her apparent negativity on the subject just encourages me onward.

"I don't care. We win some and lose some. We can't control the outcome, like you said. Let's do this," I ordered, feeling like my destiny was long ago foreseen, and my past was never meant to be a miserable, boring and worthless story, and all in vain.

"Stick around and watch, then. I might use you to assist," she concluded, smiling brightly. Charisma is not her weak point.

The process of arranging the various preparations is delightful to watch. The big center stage, the altar where Roxy had brewed up the Daerghodaemons, is the obvious focal point for the resurrection ceremony. Before long, there were colored candles burning and bright jewels and banners hung and placed all over. There is burning incense, a little something my mother used to like, I remember. Together with the dropping temperature, the darkness eventually started to become oppressive, and the comfort I felt just a moment ago was gone. I am now transcended by a deep apprehension, dare I admit fear. Facing me are a complex set of emotions I have not experienced since I saw Mother for the first time in Kangas, many years after the family collapse. I worry how all this nasty cleric business really turns out.

Roxanne begins the spell wearing her shiny, rubbery cape with that huge collar. I thought she was all gothic and stupendously attractive before, but this time I feel only dread. I feel only cold. A smoking whirlwind begins to appear on the stage, churning slowly at first, but gradually agitating itself into a torrent, not unlike the one the daerghos had earlier crawled out from. Was Mother coming up from below? My goodness, I thought she was simply dead in the natural sense. This is not what I expected, but I can now acknowledge the warnings disseminated by all the girls.

"Ulmer, hop up there and grab a hand when you see it reaching out through the maelstrom," ordered Roxy with a yell, and up I went, though I must admit I wish it were only a couple of dimwitted daerghos coming up. They were nothing but entertainment compared to what I'm feeling now. Roxanne's verbal incantation required her to rant the magic words endlessly at a shouting volume. She looked confident and intimidating, but that does not describe me. I am again humbled by this woman, I must confess.

"I see a hand!" I shouted at the very top of my voice, only to just barely be heard. The noise in here was terrific.

"Grab it and do not let go!" ordered Roxanne, and rather than Resurrection, her Deity Gate spell instigated another wave of influence that seemed to make my job easier.

With determination, and with both my hands, I grabbed a hand I knew belonged to my mother. I often looked at her hands when she tended to me at home long ago, and there are always these little things that you don't ever forget.

"Ulmer .....," came a quiet, timid voice from inside the whirlwind.

"Mother, it's me. I have you and you may come out," I said as calmly as I could.

"Ulmer, don't be angry with me, please don't be upset," she whispered quietly, possibly hoping only I would hear.

"Don't worry about anything, Mother. I'm ready," I said calmly, now feeling more confident of myself.

Something thoroughly unexpected happened just then that I will never forget, and what transpired I will never forgive. It permanently alters my perception of everything we are and disrupts my personal well-being. It was an incident I needed to have been adequately prepared for. I wish someone could have told me that this would happen, but perhaps I just did not listen.

In an instant, standing tall next to me, are my two baby step sisters Layla and Lorelei. They are bound to assist in some awful way. Both are prodigiously decked out in a bizarre kind of ceremonial costume I had never known about. They look attractively demonic and frightening, and once again I lament at my lack of a prostate. Curiosity is further empowered by the realization that Layla is brandishing a weapon, a long, serrated dagger that must be a special artifact prepared for just this ritual. I thought female clerics didn't use such weapons! How naive

I still am about so many things! Of course there are special ceremonial circumstances.

And then another thing happened. I cannot collect all my thoughts to explain this calmly. It is simply too terrible, especially for me, perhaps. Mother comes crawling out of the whirling torrent on four hairy legs. Her upper torso is naked and beautiful, another exquisite childhood memory, but her lower half is that of a ram, looking rather like a black centaur, but unkempt, jagged and daemonic, like it was summoned from the darkest chasm of Hades. This is a profound terror to behold, but it is not until she raises her head that I lose all control of my faculties. Her appearance causes me to break down in grief. Mother's head looks like that of my brother Usain. She has dozens of those same, hideous protrusions growing out of her head, face and neck. She looks like Usain, even with some of those prominences sliced clean off, but obviously this is worse, and I am beside myself with trepidation and abhorrence. No amount of healing time could ever improve this appearance, and I feel so bad for her. This is just not fair.

"Ulmer, kill me ....," she whispered as quietly as possible, hoping the others would not hear. As I alone was close enough to understand, I could only look at her in disbelief.

Just then, Roxanne began to scream orders at Layla, the first of which was more than enough for this or any other day. "Drive that dagger into Lorelei's throat right now. You refused to assist when Lorelei was born and now you must repent. Your mother died because of you! Kill your worthless sister Lorelei right now so your dear Mother Paulina may yet live and prosper!"

"No! Stop!" I screamed in protest.

"Layla, do it now! Kill Lorelei now," Roxanne ordered.

During the moments that Layla continued to hesitate, I heard another faint whisper coming from that atrocity of a creature that was supposed to be my mother.

"Ulmer, kill me now. Right now! It's the right thing. Do it now!" Mother whispered so quietly, but this time I did not fear any chance of having misunderstood. Her words were as clear in my head as anything I had ever heard her say. This was indeed Mother, if only in spirit, but a spirit that is strong and confident and of sound mind.

"Layla! Do it now! Destroy your sister!" Roxanne angrily ordered one more time, highly wound up and animated.

"No! Don't do it," I screamed, and with that rebuff, I pulled out my dagger and plunged it deep into sweet Paulina's right eye with all my strength. It went all the way in, and for the first time in our pitiful lives, I knew she was finally content and would look forward to a rest. She smiled, whispered that I was a good boy and that she loved me, and she then at last faded out forever right before me. The creature degraded into dust and was absorbed in the whirlwind. The timing was perfectly synchronized with Layla's hesitation, like it was destined to happen this way.

"Well, that was a right fucking mess, wasn't it?!" Roxanne feigned a complaint as she began to laugh. She laughed boisterously, winding herself into hysterics, like this whole scene was snipped out of some low budget comedy theater that everyone went to watch twice.

"Why did you offer it?" I screamed in anguish. "What is the meaning of all this?" I screech, protesting as loud as I could, though Roxy was obviously having her day with all this. "Why did you offer to resurrect Mother?"

"You didn't accept when I offered, Ulmer, you stupid fool! The rules change. The terms have changed! Layla refused to assist in Lorelei's birth. Everyone is responsible here! The outcome is out of my hands. These curses, Ulmer - these lasting curses - one just never knows! It's so exciting! You Ulmer - you are the only real hero here, and also the wretched idiot!" Roxanne declared at the top of her volume as she pointed directly to me, indicating my involvement must have been greater than she had guessed. Roxanne is doubtlessly enjoying all the unforeseen moments encompassing this catastrophic ritual. Every little circumstance - every apparently minor occurrence has turned into a huge surprise with monumental, permanent consequences.

But then, yet another ominous thing happens. I just cannot believe my eyes. Coming out of the whirlwind is another shape. This is the shape of one that seems to be a grown man, but not a man standing upright, rather more of a primate without any hair or skin. He has the most hideous features across his entire body. There are embroidery and jewelry literally woven into his living skeleton. Many holes are drilled into his bones, places to attach decorative jewelry and keys. He is colorfully ornamented in hideous ways. It is far beyond anything I can believe or describe. His skull and boney face are bleached completely white. There is no living tissue visible anywhere. He looks like me, but is of course less handsome, and does not possess much acumen for contemporary pop culture fashion. Usain's transformation into a lich was hard, but I see that although he struggled, a life of challenge would ultimately harden his resolve.

He begins to speak in the most irritating, scratchy voice. "Hello, my dear brother, Ulmer! I've missed you. I have come to assist. Killing mother was nice, and now for that you have me. I am in your service. You also saved Lori, my dear master! You are huge. That is fantastic! She and I are eternally attached to you, Lord and Master," the fan-dangle skeleton man explained with remarkable enthusiasm.

By this time Roxanne was calming down, and she offered a polite introduction for everyone's benefit. "Ulmer, my dear, at long last, please reacquaint yourself with your sweet brother Usain! Usain is called Ulrich now, a skilled magic-user, and he is compelled to serve. He is a present from Hades, just for you. Lori is also now obligated to you and Ulrich. Layla has forever broken bonds between herself and Lori, and you have severed all ties between you, your mother and your older sister Layla. Killing your mother for real was never anticipated.

Nobody guessed that possibility. What courage! What brilliance! You released both of them. In a way, you saved everyone, Ulmer!"

On and on Roxanne went, her hyper excited rant displaying the greatest imaginable satisfaction. It was truly an ethereal experience for everyone, but I cannot say anyone gained the same level of outright restitution as Roxanne did. For her, this was an experience to inscribe into the books for future generations of acolytes to absorb. Layla the Disgrace is miserable and disgruntled. Lori is shivering with fear, completely lost in the Darkness about what the very next move might be.

"Usain, take you sister Lorelei, and get out of here this instant. Don't ask why. Take her to the Kangas City Hall Armory and stay there until I come. You do remember where that is, don't you? How long do you need?" I boldly insisted.

"I can go this instant! I will take her there now," Ulrich said in his gravelly, crackling screech of a voice. It is the most obnoxious voice any of us have ever heard, but he seems to have risen in intelligence and is capable of some interesting magic. And with that, he laid his long, primate-like arm over to Lorelei's shoulder and they both disappeared.

By all normal measures, Paulina's resurrection was an immense catastrophe. She was an abomination to behold. And yet, in the eyes of Hades and all his minions populating the Planes of Gehenna and Tarterus, it looks like I may have saved her, that her spirit is now at peace. Some of them view this as a miserable failure, but not me. Roxy enjoyed every moment. It looks like my brother Usain is now my trusty henchman in Ulrich, and my darling little baby step-sister Lorelei is now irrevocably obliged to me. Are Roxanne and Layla satisfied with this, I wonder? I hope so, but then again, I don't really give a shit one way or the other, to be perfectly frank. I'm so done with these bitches. The boss Roxanne is cruel and sick, and I retract all previous deference to her. I stamp out all former accolades. Sister Layla is just a stupid cow, possessing not a single original thought of her own, and I have little regard for anything that basically just wastes my time.

"You made me kill my mother," I said with a sneer, directed straight at Roxanne, and no more needs to be said.

"Stupid bitch wasn't ever supposed to fucking die," Roxanne sneered back in frustration.

"Get over yourself, Roxanne. We are so done here," I concluded in anger. "You forced me to murder my own mother, you pathetic excuse for a Night Hag."

"I'll be in one day soon to collect her things, I guess," I advised toward a blank stare, the one belonging to Layla, unable to utter a word. And with that final closing remarks, I Teleport, destination set for the prearranged rendezvous point.

The Year Summarized For What It Is

I believe this must be someone else's interpretation of the Afterlife, because it sure as Hell isn't mine. I remain skeptical about its connection to me, mostly because I can sit here so calmly and talk about it. It's nothing to me, but I hope at last for Mother it is fine. I'm not the stereotypical wandering spectre of the Negative Material, roaming the Planes of Pandemonium for 600 years, getting suckered into the fire pits of Gehenna, searching for sanctity at the Gates of Tarterus and finding only Nothing. There is no need to be excessively dramatic. Searching at length for the big Nothing is what Life is all about, and I'm giving up all Hope of ever finding It. Mother discovered that a long time ago. She no longer has to look,

Considering deeply all that has happened, I am conscious of some positives that have nevertheless materialized. The outcome of Mother's resurrection was not what Roxanne and Layla had expected. I have my brother Usain back, such as he is, and despite having made no improvements in his personality or outward appearance, he possesses real power that I will exploit. He is Ulrich now, and Ulrich has Usain's courage. He will be erratic and difficult to manage at times, but a cross examination regarding his loyalty will never be required. I now have Lorelei, much to Roxy's feigned chagrin and Layla's deep-seated disgrace. She is obliged to me not only by filial family ties but also by a side effect of the curse, by Mother's assassination, and by stupid Layla's startling indifference. Ulrich and I will undeniably make good use of Lorelei as the cleric, and although she is no smoking powerhouse, she does possess the minimum of what we need. Lorelei will get better, noting how important it is that her commitment to both her step brothers is beyond reproach. Besides, who else am I getting to lick my tailbone and penetrate a slimy, drippy tongue into my right ear? The time has come to issue the final adieu to Ersa Calamy and all its bogus establishments.

Chapter 17 : The Evolution of Family Lilly

"Layla was trapped between allegiances, wasn't she," Lorelei wondered out loud.

Usain was quick to respond, screeching and scratching through the words, one at a time the way he does. "Yes, that was as good a test as we'll ever see. She will not remain obligated to anyone from today onward. It must have been a long-awaited objective of hers, and right then and there, she was presented the opportunity."

"The truth will blow in the wind for a while. I cannot Commune on it or everyone will know. We are strongly interdependent below, and the myriad of connections among Hades' cohorts and sub-dukes and vassals and daemons will be forever duplicitous, even traitorous! That will never change," warned Lorelei.

"Let's dig some ways into the implications," I insisted. "Layla disobeyed her mentor and severed that relationship. That took some guts on her part because Roxanne has a propensity to hold grudges. I know that now, finding out the hard way. She raked our mother over the glowing embers. She dragged her through the raging fire to atone for the endless perceived insurrections, and also for those committed by our half-witted grandfather who couldn't keep his greasy mitts off Roxanne. He was the sucker and I almost was, too. Roxanne hated our mother and intended to keep her in permanent torment. Roxy did not expect a point blank assassination. I am sorry about that, but we must accept that it is the least of all our evils, a dominating side effect of the Darkness we have created around ourselves. Lori, Layla is no longer your mentor so Usain and I will take care of you. You now have your wings."

"I am at your service, dear brother. Mom has her wings, too," Lorelei declared.

"I admit I must also have begun with an uncontrollable infatuation for Roxanne at first. I am sorry about that, too," I lamented in earnest.

"We told you so, didn't we, Layla and I. Roxanne is very difficult to ignore. I never could have broken away if it had not been for your and Layla's massive indiscretion. Mom's condition at the Gate was probably way out of Roxanne's hands by then, but I suppose, dear brother, you could then fully appreciate her true character. She is powerful and complicated, and above all absolutely has to be your enemy. You cannot continue to be a victim of her charm, as powerful and as fantastic as you think those charms may be. Roxanne will always need to be on top, and when the ripened fruit is firmly in her hands, she squeezes the juice out to the last fucking drop. She rends it with a twist that sucks it completely dry, an attitude that frightens every Lord of the Underworld. She will not suffer subservience or allegiance to anyone except our Dark Lord Hades himself. She aims to stand at his side regardless of the cost. Anyway, if it's any consolation, dear brother, it is entirely your green light to hold a grudge in return. Lord Hades will love the intrigue!" confided Lorelei in detail, and what a tale it is.

"I worry about the choices placed before Baby Sister Layla at this time. She is faced with a dilemma of unprecedented magnitude. She might fall from evil grace, or she might be actively seeking help, or she might go off alone, or - or she might go suck-holing to Roxanne ," I realized out loud, recognizing how all the possible outcomes are plenty for us to worry about.

This is the first time I have heard Lorelei rise up and grab the ripening fruit. I have facilitated her establishment and she is no longer in a cage. The only question is where home shall be, where she might establish. Although I cannot speak for the cleric, I have ideas to present.

Kangas will not do because the growing interest from all rival pantheons will compel us to pack up. At some point, we would be compelled to leave. The Peninsula of Hate is the obvious long range choice, but for now countless unknowns still exist there, and a huge amount of work lies ahead. I am ready to decide on something I hinted at years ago: I am ready to move back to the beloved Hallucinatory Sanctuary of Cirsalsomere. From there we can work.

In no time at all, the RILF is set up and ready to become home once again. The scenery is of a dusty, stony landscape sparsely covered with dead trees. That hasn't changed. My earlier magic did not aim to beautify the landscape. But today, a barrage of new illusion spells go all the way to appropriating the magical premises into a comfortable home. The house and yard get plenty of treatments that improve our comfort and confuse everyone else. The house feels much larger and far better appointed than when I was here alone, and quickly demonstrates its adequacy for two crazy wizards and one highly-polished person of prayer. The female touch proved useful.

Lorelei found great difficulty at first getting used to the endless array of Permanent illusions all about the land, but she wasn't alone. Several rival bands of gnolls and an army of orcs had wandered in within the last year and gotten themselves permanently dazed and confused. A handful of trolls are running around aimlessly, cursing and muttering to themselves, scoffing at one another in frustration and confusion. It is amusing to sit back and watch what happens when those bone-headed trolls bump into gnolls. Everyone is angry, agitated and argumentative and the scene quickly descends into a bar brawl typical of a daily event in Milan's Southwest precinct. All this perplexity and bewilderment assisted Lori with learning her way around, and she developed creative new applications for her Truth of Sight. Usain was politely manipulated into procuring an obsidian statue of The Dark Lord, a Scrying Font, an Unholy Fountain, an Unholy Water Basin and an ornate Altar of Hades. The little spring fortifying The Marshes of Nulwong has now been given a whole new lease on its existence. Lorelei had not ever had these provisions in her own name, deferring to her mentor in all matters, and we quickly recognize how she might some day come to eclipse her own mentor in capabilities. But such arrangements are basic. In late 692, a Wish is still considered adequate to facilitate the tools she longs for, resources with which to forge her destiny. Lorelei is grateful now for the choices I have been forced to make on everyone's behalf and pledges to make the best use out of the advantages placed before her. On this point, I am forced to humbly admit that some things were only a matter of good fortune. I have determined to adopt Lorelei as a legal dependent, and am now officially permitted to refer to her as my sister, Lorelei Lilly. We agree it is an astonishingly good name, especially when a surname simply did not previously exist at all. Will there one day be a Layla Lilly, we wonder? It would be nice.

A good boss knows how to delegate, and each of us have thus been saddled with a major task best suited to our aptitudes and objectives. Usain can play as tough as Ulrich demands now, and since his destiny has been proclaimed by the greatest of influencers living in the Darkness far below, he will soon be adept at showing one face to us and another to the world. To us he is and will always be our very dearest Usain Lilly. Lorelei is acutely bewitched by Usain's remarkable duplicity, and not only by his benign side facing us. She laments that the Daemon Lords of Gehenna have not matured to such an exalted state and wonders how he has done it. I conclude it is all about the power of freedom and the ability to exercise free will.

Usain and I will part company for a while. I have delegated a huge project that will keep him employed for the best part of the next two years, possibly more if unexpected hurdles are presented.

Ulrich is tasked with the massive job of constructing a safety mechanism in each tomb at The Peninsula of Hate. Exactly how it is expected to function eludes me at this point, but a lengthy perusal of a map depicting the typical Tomb Configuration will provide clues to its general design and construction. I am the architect but not its engineer. Mosaics in the wall and on the floor synchronized together with automated portcullis gates will be part of the prescription in place there, and having extra security around the lich laboratories will be required.

Lorelei is working on two simultaneous and equally important objectives. She cannot adventure alone as she does not yet possess the clerical skill of Teleport Recall, but she is getting very close. She is tasked with the job of setting up two Hades Sanctuaries, one of which needs to be with us here in Cirsalsomere, right inside the RILF. Whether the Sanctuary itself can be portable remains to be seen, and what happens when RILF is in transit is also as yet unclear, but as long as the fortress is deployed, Teleport Recall is expected to work perfectly. I had it previously deployed right here, and lived nicely in it for seven uninterrupted years!

Lorelei's other big job is assisting Ulrich at his work. Life without a cleric at his side could be troublesome, but allowing them to work together lets me feel confident that great things are destined to come. There will be times when I need to tap into their skills, and times when further delegation and updates are required, so weekly rendezvous at prearranged times are set to take place right here.

My job is another story, and it might be a long one. Its success has no guarantees.

Chapter 18 : The Hand and The Eye

Tansiméta

"Feel free to ask for whatever I may grant you," instructed the same middle-aged female figure, far older than appearances suggest, standing on the same timeless platform, dressed in the usual ceremonial attire. Her arms are fully extended with hands at waist height, palms face up and held out toward me. This gesture confides a memory of who I am. She also said "whatever" this time, a little thing that took me by surprise, though I cannot pin down its significance.

"Hello, Dearest Lady Tansiméta. I hope you've been well," I said, feeling like an idiot, realizing such small talk has no meaning to an oracle, especially not this oracle.

"No point worrying about me, but your concern is noted. What may I grant you?" she asked.

"I'm on the search yet again for The Hand and The Eye of Hades. I have misplaced both items now," I said.

"Those items are not available," she said plainly.

My stomach turned itself upside down in an instant. I feel like vomiting. What does that mean, not available? "I'm sorry, please let me clarify. The items cannot be obtained because they are not here? Is that correct?"

"The items are not here," she frankly stated.

"I thank you for the information. I'm sorry to waste your time," I said.

"Time is all I have and it cannot therefore be wasted," she declared, and the oracle disappeared.

Well, that was short. It is a very long journey for such a short chat, but the profundity of knowledge gained makes me want to do it more often. I know of no living person who can engage in efficient conversation equal to Tansiméta.

Lorelei Helps Out At Raulston's

It is becoming increasingly clear to me that I will never be allowed an easy way past this Fred G. Gearbox character. Every time I go out of my way to avoid or ignore him, he's there making a goofy face, right in my face. Every time I attempt a productive collaboration with him, he runs and hides, straight down the rabbit hole. He wants nothing to do with me. Every time the subject of Raulston comes up, or anything even remotely pertaining to him, The Gearbox rolls up his sleeves and gets into my hair. I knew years ago we had a connection. He knew it, too. But this nonsensical song and dance is ridiculous and I will not suffer it.

I now speculate these Milanese assassinations have us connected even tighter. The implications of these actions are deeply rooted in both of us. They connect us to each other and to the Milan underworld. I wonder whether The Hand and The Eye might be behind this to some extent, influencing our decisions and manipulating our actions. Certainly they are a common denominator. Perhaps it is only Fred pulling the strings, but I have my doubts about that. He hasn't been around as long. If I sound frustrated and angry, I apologize. I am frustrated. But an apology doesn't address the issues that I have. At some point I'm going to have to confront or engage the Gearbox in some way. And I realize I might be delusional; those relics were all my idea after all.

Teleporting home to sunny and beautiful Cirsalsomere, to the RILF, where no normal, living mortal would willingly choose to reside, I stop for a moment to marvel at the device we call home. I am ready to rename it ULF, Ulmer's Little Fortress, a name that is bound to have significant consequences for all of us going forward. I love the concept of leaving the future of all things wide open and unpredictable. There can be vast destiny in all things, and unexpected opportunities might arise at any time. But if nothing happens in the end, a pile of weak sarcasm is all we have left to fall back on for amusement.

On the predetermined meeting time, Usain and Lori pop in exactly on schedule, but frustrated with having to comply with bureaucratic duties, Usain is given a pass to return to his efforts at The Peninsula of Hate.

Lori stays with me. The provisional Scrying Font and Hades Altar are satisfactory resources, and with them we set ourselves into an extensive reconnaissance mission. The single pair of Deity Commune and Scrying Font spells utterly maximize the extent of Lori's daily capacity, but it is enough, as I have previously declared, and the contribution warrants a reassuring word or two to avoid embarrassment. With healthy doses of leniency, clemency and patience, she'll get to where she wants.

We peer into the neighborhood surrounding the abode of my former mentor, hoping to catch a glimpse of the G making his way around. This proves to be an arduous task as we do not well predict his activities, and therefore instead choose to double up on Deity Commune one day to get a deeper look into his daily life. The revised strategy evinces excellent performance, and in just three days we manage to learn everything we need to know about the dude. He isn't that deep. A planned outing with Kadrah leaves his place unattended for several days. He's buried the premises in layers of stupendous illusions that would send anyone running off in terror, anyone except Lorelei and me, that is. When we're confident all is clear, we teleport in.

I can see what items have interested The G and what he has ignored. There are certain items, still in their usual old places, that would hold a strong bond between my mentor and I, were he still around. I can clearly identify the abrasions on his desktop, created when he sawed his left hand off. There are two magic artifacts of particular interest to me, two things the G has neither discovered nor identified. The G-Man will likely not miss these items and I'm helping myself to them. Just for fun, I'm also taking a very valuable rock he will right away notice missing so I'll make it look like Thieves Guild Members were the culprits. I want to see how he retaliates when he discovers the disappearance of a single enchantable gem worth 30,000 gold pieces.

Lorelei does an Object Location and finds nothing. The Hand and The Eye are not here and moments later we are back in Cirsalsomere.

Lorelei Helps Out At Home

I have another idea. A Deity Commune next day lets us focus on learning the recent fate of The Hand and The Eye, and very few questions are needed to learn they are once again both on Gehenna 2. This time however, they are not in the possession of the dynamic-duo Daerghos. They are in the possession of their bosses, a pair of self-righteous Arcanadaemons whose names elude us. Doing her research with diligence and efficiency, Lori advises superior daemons will do whatever it takes to keep their real names and any official, ceremonial names a secret. Resourcefulness being a particular skill of my own, I employ an Alter Reality to know that I know the official names of two Arcanadaemons living together on Gehenna 2. Same as with the Daerghos, the usual place of residence would be found in The Glooms of Hades, but for reasons of clandestine motives, secrecy or banishment, Gehenna and Tarterus could also serve as suitable residences for daemons. How many pairs of Arcanadaemons can there really be on Gehenna 2? I will wager this 30,000 gold piece rock these two run the show there.

The Arcanadaemons dominating our consciousness are Deyagora and Goradeya, a twin pair who promote the virtues of public incest among their kind and among all their subjugated followers. In

Gehenna and Tarterus, no one ever does anything willingly, but a public display of incest is one exception. D & G are bipedal creatures with the heads of jackals or hyenas or some other derelict species of quasi-canine vermin. Deciding which the effector is and which the recipient is, quickly descends into a heated argument as their androgynous nature makes it tricky to find distinctions. Lorelei considers it a genre of black humor, if you can believe that, though she admits to being an old-fashioned conservative. But honestly, we are getting too carried away; we really have no first hand experience with any of this, and it's time to stop musing over this nonsense and get serious.

Lorelei pleads for an uninterrupted week to prepare herself for the unstated destination. She plans to write two Plane Shifting scrolls, two Truth of Sight scrolls and three Walking on Air scrolls to pad her limited capabilities of high level spells. Since Usain isn't expected to return for six days, the timing works out well.

But six days do not prove sufficient. Some weeks pass and we find ourselves months into 693, long before we realized the passage of any time at all. Time is of concern to Demi liches only, evinced by the fact that Lori used up much more than the one week we had originally discussed, and Usain flat out failed to show up for four consecutive weekly progress meetings. I don't know whether to commend them for diligence or shit on them for delinquency. Being the boss is sometimes like being placed in difficulty, so for now I will assume both are deferring to our highest intentions. The simple fact is I need to be realistic about how long things take. Clearly, I am the one who does not understand!

Usain and Lorelei Thrive Deep Below

Once we are together at last, they both end up surprising me with a level of insight I had not prepared for. After a good rest and a days-long session of idolatry, Lorelei and Usain both bid ready.

Lori was first up. "These Heat Resistances will allow us to withstand the 160-degree F temperature. We might even enjoy it."

Usain began screeching in a most annoying way, as though he had in his prolonged weeks of silence forgotten how to talk. He did however, manage to impress.

"I was down on Hades 1 for some time before you brought me back, no idea how long it was. Time has no meaning there. I measured the atmosphere of Gehenna 2 to have a whopping 3.5% carbon dioxide. As far as I know, there are 3% sulfur dioxide and a dangerously meager 6% oxygen in its atmosphere. I'm working on a way to fix that for us, otherwise we will not be comfy, trust me. Most biological life forms cannot tolerate more than the lethal limit of around 4% carbon dioxide, and only if oxygen were at least 20%, which it obviously isn't. I'll be fine. The bigger problem is the gravity. It's 40% higher than what we have evolved to, and comes at a five-degree slant because of the funky geology. There is a super dense, ultra heavy metallic core slightly offset from center that makes everything we do difficult. Even walking is difficult. Casting spells with semantics is nearly impossible for us, but not for them. I'm fixing all that right now," Usain explained, and I could right away recognize the Herculean strength of his magic unleashed, the Limited Wishes he was invoking to correct these handicaps for us and hopefully turn the tide.

It is so comforting, even refreshing if I may say, to witness Usain functioning at this level. I always somehow imagined it. I knew such great possibility was there. I wonder now whether the curse simply prevented him from physically expressing himself, that his intellect was all along buried deep inside himself, unattainable by all others, myself included. His time growing up was deeply frustrating from another perspective I had not fully registered before. Maybe Mom knew it and kept it to herself. It's too late to go there. I'm not about to start pointing fingers at her after all that has happened. I have a better idea.

Lorelei ordered us to stand close while holding hands. A scroll was produced and in a few moments the appropriate tuning fork was sounded. Gehenna 2 proved to be everything we had wished for and more. Lori did not especially appreciate the prodigious weight gain, but the slightly slanted gravity did let my rib jewels hang in a way that added a touch of ornamental panache and a corresponding dollop of charisma, if only to my eyes. Usain just walked with a crippled gait that reminded me of an aging primate, or even a prehistoric human, but then I wondered what if anything had actually changed.

The heat is stifling, 150 degrees F at least. No water can be seen anywhere. The sky is a deep orange, closer to darkness than daylight, and the atmosphere is dense and odorous. The land consists of endlessly jagged, black volcanic mountains with vertical cliffs. Violent eruptions and lava flows are all around in all directions. Sometimes a vent will appear out of nowhere and spew molten magma at surprising distances and direction. It makes sense never to get too close to anything attached to this plane, but taking into consideration the broad advantages offered by our magic, we are able to function normally.

"I like it here. It feels strangely comfortable," admitted Usain.

"Ewww, not me! I gained, like twenty pounds! My baby skeleton wasn't meant to support such a pig!" complained Lori. This time she was the one doing the screeching. I can understand, but given the counterbalances issued by our magic, I felt she might have exaggerated a little. We are going to be just fine, you'll see.

"Now it is time to get serious," I warned, as we reached the end of a narrow ravine and entered a flat, roughly circular region possibly a mile or more across. The area is completely closed in and surrounded by vertical, jagged rock cliffs. Open pits and smoking vents exist across its entire expanse, and visibility is nearly zero. The amount of caution needed to avoid falling into one would frustrate an army and destroy any meaningful military strategy. To address these conditions, Lorelei brings out the second of her homework efforts, three Walking On Air scrolls that eliminate the current handicap. She judiciously explains why the spell requires dexterity to maintain balance, and lots of time getting accustomed to, so we must not attempt any brave stunts until we have experienced at least five durations. Usain, not being particularly well endowed with dexterity, decides to sit down in order to safely present the next installment to our cause. His next Limited Wish compelling the Arcanadaemons Deyagora and Goradeya to conclude we will surely not be defeatable in a fight and my Alter Reality to place us within sight of their home accelerate our mission in the most efficient and businesslike manner.

I'm really starting to enjoy Gehenna, like even maybe choose to reside here some day. Such a decision would surely rank up my advantage against some rivals.

"Why have you come?" both Daemons asked in stereo, speaking closely together but in separate bass and baritone octaves.

Although quite evil looking with fiery red eyes, they are surprisingly polite. One looks like a hyena, the other a mangy wolf of some type. Both stand as robed, bipedal humans in all other apparent characteristics including their hands, a feature that makes poor Usain appear demonic by comparison. He is a lich after all.

"We would like to recover our property," I said plainly. "We have come to beg for your kindness, your goodwill and common sense. We must acquire The Hand and The Eye of our Master for an important purpose, the fruits of which we may share in equal weight," I added, pretending to appeal with a naive innocence. It was a lie, of course, and I don't yet know exactly how much Usain's spell is contributing, but for now it feels better to go easy. We'll see how this goes. Obviously it can spiral out of control at any moment.

"They have been asking for you. We have tried to reason with them. We tried to mold them into our frame without success. If you want them, you may have them, but we ask for a twenty-five percent royalty on all your achievements," responded either Deyagora or Goradeya - I don't know which is which.

The candor and civility of these dudes surprise me. I was ready for something else, and this is certainly as much of a performance on their part as it is on mine, but let's remember Roxy and how these things can suddenly change. For the time being, our magic influences beyond anyone's manipulation or control and I decide to milk it some more.

"I see. I regret the need to counter the percentage, for it is a little spicy. Let's agree upon a ten-percent royalty on all our achievements, and I offer this stone today as a good-faith deposit," I said as I produced the gem I filched from Raulston's. Their eyes lit up as I casually tossed it over to them, confident that one would easily catch it, but they didn't, an interesting point that I must remark upon in detail.

The gem went plunging down a narrow, vertical vent, straight into the smoking blackness. Through Psionic Telekinesis, I grab ahold of it before the molten rock below exacts its danger. I feel a slight mental tug-of-war when both Daemons do the same, and it becomes apparent they value the gem more than I could have hoped. In that same immediate moment Usain, recognizing an opportunity to change the landscape, Dimension Portals out to an unknown location, and in the next moment we see him floating around, looking down the vent where he believes the rock has fallen. I believe I can deduce what he has done, and before I give away the farm with a bad dice roll, I need to ascertain what the Daemons can understand, assuming any time is available for the others to understand anything at all, and that even includes Lori. I must concentrate on that stone for a moment, not that I care about it so much, but rather my psionic attention to it keeps them occupied. I see now what has happened, and I am ready to disclose a secret of unmatched proportions. We are locked in a Time Stoppage.

I have never imagined this feeling. It lasts no more than a minute and a half, but I swear it feels like a hundred years. The Daemons and

I are locked onto the gem with our Psionic Telekinesis, but there is nowhere to go with it. There is nothing for anyone to do except stare.

That goes for anyone except Usain. In the next moment, I realize that the Usain we see floating around, pretending to look into vents, feigning concern over that gem, is not Usain at all, but an Image Projection of himself. Nobody knows exactly where he is, and in the very next second following, four flaming balls, each maybe two feet in diameter appear from the fingers of his Image Projection, and explode point blank against the hyena Daemon, whichever one he is. It is a Swarm of Meteors, a spell that utterly destroys Deyagora and leaves Goradeya at the mercy of Usain's wishes.

All this has happened without any particular cause. Usain has acted in an aggressive manner, demonstrating the single most evil intent I have yet witnessed from him. I'm reminded of forgettable days in our miserable childhood in Kangas some thirty years ago. This is just a natural progression for him, if I may say, given a general acknowledgment of his improved capabilities. He has at last embodied the character of the monster that has been prescribed to him all along. He is Ulrich the Lich, and with mentorship not from me but from the Darkness below, cannot be answerable to anyone above, and that has to include me.

Goradeya is pleased to hand over The Hand and The Eye in exchange for his life and for dominion over the land. We take extra care to transfer them safely to our transport device, trying extra hard not to handle or concentrate on them. Goradeya had been awarded a promotion. He is now the Boss of around half of the Gehenna 2 Daemonic realm, as well as becoming an ally of ours, a vassal to command however we require. Together with The Relics of our Master, we also extorted forty thousand mithril coins and an archived copy of Deyagora's Book of Magic. All else shall remain as is for Goradeya to own and rule as he desires. He will need more than just money to govern his realm alone, but he is satisfied with how things have turned out. The one thing that did not go as planned: the thirty thousand gold piece stone melted into the magma, returning all the way back to the roots of its creation.

Usain and The Hand and The Eye

"Let's do one each, brother! Which one do you want?" Usain began with an overly enthusiastic screech.

"Let's take our time to consider it carefully," I suggested.

Lorelei was much less eager to jump in. "Why are you two lump heads in such a hurry? Do you not realize the implications these relics present to our objectives? Didn't Roxanne warn you again and again about them? Did you not recognize the profound effects they had on Raulston? You thought he was in your control, but was he really? I don't think so," ranted Lorelei. I admit she isn't wrong.

Just then we agreed we heard a faint but highly dimensional whisper from the relics and I decide to keep them covered up and out of sight. Lorelei is correct. She advises how we must not enter into this chapter hastily. There are terrible consequences without any shred of recourse. And then, as I consider Lorelei's wisdom more thoroughly, I begin to doubt Usain. I don't doubt his loyalty. I doubt his capacity to reason and his limited ability to make sound choices. These are not evil traits by any measure, but rather an immaturity he has so far never grown out of. The Hand and The Eye can detect and influence this type of weakness and will surely attempt to exploit it. Both artifacts have egos that can rival or complement each other as the desire arises, and this kind of unpredictability makes them dangerous. As so, after a considerable debate with myself, I make a decision. Much to Lorelei's obvious satisfaction and Usain's calm chagrin, in complete confidence I employ an Alter Reality to hide the relics from all knowledge and methods of location. They shall lie in silence for another day.

Chapter 19 : Layla

"I'm getting worried about Layla," Lorelei came out of the blue with, on a day the three of us were together in Cirsalsomere, several weeks after the Gehenna journey. It is unclear whether it was based on fact or just a feeling between sisters, a hunch between clerics.

"Can we Commune on it?" I wondered, even while realizing the risk has probably not subsided.

"That is still not a recommendable action. We should consider going quietly down to Ersa Calamy and pop into the Temple unannounced. I still have an assortment of possessions to pick up, giving me some excuse to show up there. I don't know whether she's made peace with Roxy, and I wonder what her ambitions are. She might be overjoyed to see us, or she might just want to blast the Unholy Utterance. Anything is possible. Not sure exactly what good that would do, but those emotions are not difficult to understand," deliberated Lorelei out loud.

"Can we forge an alliance with her that is guaranteed, or is her life another Roxanne in process? What are your thoughts? Should we try to welcome her into our group?" I asked, looking for any kind of honest advice. I'm good at deferring to my team on matters they excel at.

Usain was quick to pipe in there with a tail-winded story all his own. "I wonder maybe it would be fruitless. Layla deeply despises me. She considers my mere existence utterly contemptible. I could feel an intense repugnance from her the very first moment I was sent back through Roxy's Gate. She loathes the fact that I'm here and Mother is dead. I am the sick and demented consolation prize. It is so hard to wrap my mind around the understanding that all four of us have the same mother! No Ulmer, I think she hates us boys - but not you Lori; she loves you, I know it. But she torments herself having no official hold over you. She hates you Ulmer, for killing mother. In her mind, you had to come up with another course of action to be the satisfactory leader. Layla refused to kill Lori, a point that forever put her in bad rapport with her mentor Roxanne, and so she wishes you hadn't assassinated mother! She feels somehow morally superior, as if that means anything. I don't actually know anything! It's all my perception only!"

"Well, let's go see for ourselves, all three of us together so there is no misunderstanding," I ordered, and when I make a decision, no more needs to be said about it.

In the late night urban darkness, every street torch is lit and Ersa Calamy doesn't disappoint. Streets are busy with markets, merchants, buyers, jugglers, buskers, beggars and thieves. Even in the wee hours, there is no shortage of activity or entertainment, a feature that Lori has missed, judging by her smile. There is plenty of food available for everyone at low prices, a condition that illuminates the city's economic resourcefulness and prosperity. Ersa Calamy near the dawn of another day 694 is pretty great, while in contrast Milan requires comparative compromises, and I expect it to get worse.

"What the fuck do all of you want? Be on your way now, bye-bye. I have no desire for any of you!" exclaimed Layla in protest right off.

Today is the first time since Mom's ceremonial assassination that I have fixated upon Layla, already some five months ago. She does not seem the least thrilled to see us, making Usain's predictions appear accurate. What I notice, apart from the fact that she no longer worships me, is her appearance. She is sinking lower in measure of charisma, as though beauty is now evaluated on an alternative scale.

"You went sucking up to Roxanne, didn't you, Layla," I sneered at her with a biting remark that got looks of wonder from the others.

"Well, what did you expect? You sold me out even when I did my best. Anyway, Roxanne does not own me. I severed her hold over me at that critical moment," she remarked in mild revolt, sounding a little embarrassed. Her volume has already lowered.

"We do not doubt your consideration, Sister. We doubt your ability to apply sound reasoning going forward. Your new appearance makes me think you have either been cursed or forced into a difficult circumstance. Ass kissing that deranged Night Hag up the street wasn't wise," I retorted.

Lorelei also felt an urgent need to say something. "Roxanne is no longer in our best interest. She will never concede anything to our Family interests. She abhors everything to do with the name Lilly. I thank you so much, dear Sister, my dear Mentor, for saving me in that critical moment. I am responsible for your troubled situation. I am so sorry about it," she confided.

By now both sisters were in tears as they hugged each other, and I even thought Usain was struck with a moment of tenderness. Still, the hand gesture from him mimicking a hatchet chop to the neck suggests he feels no warmth from her and is counting the seconds before he disappears. He knows better, though he believes that making things right with Layla on a personal level seems unrealistic, at least for now.

Layla started a long explanation. "I must tell you that Roxanne has been preoccupied with your activities since that Day. We were together quite often for some weeks, and she revealed to me that following you had become quite the obsession of hers. Roxy had long been connected with the Arcanadaemons you subjugated, and Goradeya was quick to report to her what happened. He is desperately afraid of her power and influence. I am to lose my title as Matriarch of Sodon Calamy. I am her pawn. I am going to Gehenna to live with Goradeya. We will always somehow be connected I suppose, but maiden family ties will be considered secondary. Goradeya and I will simultaneously have to answer to both you and Roxanne, and I see plenty of interesting times ahead, like who says what to whom and when. Lorelei, you are now Matriarch of Sodon Calamy, and my Temple, indeed your former home, is yours. I am done here," Layla declared.

"You could still join us. We would be very strong together," I offered with the minimum of encouragement.

"I appreciate the thought. I won't rule anything out in the future, whether together or apart, but the terms laid before me to become Goradeya's cohort are extremely attractive. I shall consider it a mid-level promotion and perhaps, if I keep my head down, we'll be able to communicate in writing, viewing through a Scrying Font. No verbal sounds are possible and I'll destroy each message. Let's set this exact day and time for monthly contact. More often is better but let's not push our luck at first," Layla advised.

We all agreed on the proposed plan. Layla had a very fast, if not instantaneous turn-around, and seems content. Fragmenting our relations might have been Roxanne's hope, and normally it would have worked, but we are the deeply connected Family Lilly and sometimes that matters. The girls had one more sisterly intimacy and we departed by the slowest way available. It's a great chance to reacquaint ourselves with a hectic urban lifestyle. We made ourselves merry sampling the various cafés and theaters disguised in Self Change illusions. There is no pressing need to hurry and a little enjoyable procrastination is great for our morale.

Getting Lori moved back into our former home is a simple task. A few quick trips to ULF and back are all that is required. She decides to leave many of her things at ULF and therefore manages a permanent satellite destination with us. She can come wherever we are and whenever she chooses. It's a great advantage and while we're here, we look forward to sleeping in Layla's giant satin bed once again. Usain will use Lori's old room when we visit and that's as close to sniffing the sheets as he'll be permitted to get. For him it is the definition of luxury and I'm glad.

We decide to stay in Ersa Calamy for a while, assist with whatever Layla requires on her way out, and generally work to nurture the family bond. After a few quiet and comfortable days doing nothing but lounging about eating Layla's Banquet of Heroes, she stopped leering and sneering at Usain by the end. Usain had never eaten that before, and it seemed as though he was elevated to some higher state of being. Layla was moved. Much of our time together was spent being lazy and a huge amount of relief, camaraderie and goodwill was shared all around. It is the further evolution of the Family Lilly and one that we hope cannot be challenged. I am satisfied and pledge to remain optimistic for Layla's endeavors and good fortune. Meanwhile, Lori goes straight to prayer and idolatry, sensing something big is just about to happen to her as well. We are going to be fine.

Chapter 20 : Two Infamous Transformations

The Analysis

Usain was restless. In thirty days, he had made thirty trips to the Peninsula of Hate. As his work there was reaching an important landing worthy of a full progress report, I went with him one day to witness for myself what was happening there, what he was so diligently preoccupied with. Let me summarize by declaring Usain the right dude for the job. He went on and on about this and that, details best left for another tale, but on some matters I am ashamed to declare myself the man in charge. I pretend. I miss Lori too, some days, though there is just a single word between us and excuses therefore need not be made.

The first planned Scrying Font meeting at Lori's went well and nobody bothered anyone with unpleasant news. Confirming we could do it as well as expected was a source of considerable satisfaction to us all. One advantage to writing messages for viewing is we have time to think about what we want to say, and efficiencies matter when you have time constraints. Lorelei declares her new ability to create Feasts of Heroes and Barriers of Blades, Heal All Injuries and Teleport Recall, any one of those precisely once per day. Layla strongly advises regular adventuring to be prudent now, otherwise sedentary behavior postpones the acquisition of the Devil Exaction and The Unholy Utterance unreasonably long. We schedule the next bipolar Font meeting at this precise one-month interval.

"It's just you and me now. I miss the girls already," remarked Usain, just two days after our business trip to The Peninsula together.

"Me, too. It is nice having them close by, especially when there are no issues," I agreed.

Within just a week, Layla softened on Usain very dramatically, much to our relief. She took a moment to correctly perceive his true character and unflinching loyalty to Paulina, our Mom and to all things concerning Lilly. I was glad for her acknowledgement, because for all the awful things that happened, nothing was ever Usain's fault. He was simultaneously the weakest pawn and the biggest victim, and not once did he ever whine or object. He is the rock we must all strive to be if we are to prosper.

"What are we going to do now?" he asked with an impatience that suggests he's ready for some serious fun.

"Are you thinking what I'm thinking?" I wondered.

"What are you thinking, brother? If you're thinking what I think you're thinking, we'd better be careful - and methodical," Usain mused. His tone is rather diabolical, and I feel myself sinking again as well.

"You're right. I've thought long and hard about Roxanne's warnings. On one hand, she wanted me to remain manageable, malleable and compliant. That way she would always have her heavy thumb pressed firmly upon my forehead, and she would not be faced with any meaningful resistance. But also there was a unintended hidden truth in her warnings. She flatly refused to consider any personal involvement with them, a point that made me understand how clear her vision is, and also how treacherous the artifacts are to realizing one's objectives. And then there was the Raulston experiment, poor guy. I used my own mentor as a laboratory specimen, and he went down in profound despair. You missed out; we'll review the whole scenario for your benefit. What I can deduce is how the artifacts might assist with our needs and objectives, and I see something quite different from Roxanne," I explained to a very eager countenance seated before me.

And so at last comes what is arguably the most important milestone in our lives, indeed across generations within the Family Lilly. All three girls have chosen conservative, methodical approaches to their professions. I stipulate that is what clerics are expected to do and everything will eventually work out for them within their chosen paths.

Usain and I are however, destined for a very different road. There are no expectations. Ever since our miserable, pathetic Kangas childhood, there have never been expectations, not by anyone alive. This now becomes our strength, when the powers that exist do not see us coming. We decide to employ The Hand and The Eye of Hades ourselves, allocating one piece each. Usain will work with The Eye and I will attempt to forge whatever relationship I can with The Hand. While there is very limited recourse for changing our minds when we become unhappy, we intend to administer a strict game plan that will afford several important advantages. Considering the amount of experimentation and deliberation I've already invested into this, I can easily decide our course. We might stack the odds in our favor from the beginning. These things I learned from The Raulston Experiment. I love the name.

"Usain, I want you to listen to me carefully. I am going first. You haven't had nearly enough exposure. I need you to witness the terrible transformation process and from that, you'll see what eventually happens to you. Once my hand transformation has begun, The Eye will begin taunting us both day and night. You must not give in to its power for at least say, six months to a year. You must look after me at all costs. This is priority one. You see, I will go completely mad and make a lot of people very, very angry. I'll invite a retaliation of enormity and I will probably be crippled. Look what happened to Raulston. He thought he was invincible, and then the artifacts, predicting his weakness, sold him out for what was supposed to be a better game. That's where we came and unexpectedly altered destiny. Your mission is to shadow me wherever I go, and rescue me from whatever befalls me. Get Lorelei to help with Deity Communes and Scrying Fonts, and definitely inform Layla. She'll make chasing me around a passion. We did precisely this with Raulston to huge effect so the girls already know the procedure. Raulston was all over the place. Rox the Night Ox can obsess over it all on her own. I'm no longer concerned with what she does."

"That is easy to understand. How do I know when it's my turn to take the plunge?" Usain eagerly asked.

"There are two likely scenarios. One is if anything bad happens to me, and you and the girls have done everything within reason to correct the situation, but nothing works. Making your Eye transformation will instantly create an intense bond between us. The Hand and The Eye will obligate you to get the job done, however you can, by whatever means available. The girls will not like it, so don't expect a lot of sympathy once you go there. Note that if we both get irreversibly traumatized, it's game over and the artifacts will aggressively seek new hosts. Obviously, that mustn't happen. So if I get into deep shit, you must fix it and keep yourself out of trouble."

"What's the second?" he asked, right in tune with my thoughts.

"The opposite case is when things are going really well - if we have no major worries, no troubles. In that case we might together decide and go berserk," I said, jokingly. "I expect the first case to be more likely, but you never know. Your other important task is to keep the sisters on side. That might be more difficult than it sounds, especially if things get tough to control. We cannot again allow Layla to go astray. Not ever! Family Lilly is now in a renaissance and we honor our parents. Goradeya will treat her like a queen, I expect, but if not, you and Lorelei will obviously have to correct the situation, obviously better to keep Layla loyal. My guess is she will suffer everything except the crazy weight gain!" We had a good laugh over that.

Many more weeks of study and meditation go by. Usain reports the creation of three important apprentices, squeezed out from the Kangas leadership I manipulated Raulston into creating during his campaign there. Lorelei visits us once or twice a week, always keeping a back-up Teleport Recall scroll in case of an emergency. By our fifth scheduled Font Scry, I acknowledge both Layla and Lorelei's advancement in power and status, and by the middle of 694, note Lorelei's long-standing habit of carrying those reserve scrolls is in systemic decline.

Layla has had more than her share of issues in Gehenna. Power struggles forced an authoritative coup d'état against Goradeya's questionable leadership. That presented her with the need to get busy improving herself and she is making strides during this time. Lori also assists with emergency trips to Gehenna as needed. As I have said before, two like-minded clerics are infinitely better than one.

I am satisfied with my Team. I'm already calling them My Team, though it's usually the clerics that have that privilege. Look at who are actually in charge at Team Hades, Team Dionysus and Team Zeus. Why should I care about any of them? They are all a bunch of second rate hacks and I will have no serious road block.

The Plunge in Mid-694

I will excel.

I will amaze everyone with a whole new version of shock and awe. Family is expected to be involved in some of that surprise, but that is not my intention. Harassing my own is not part of the mission. I must confide in Layla and Lorelei about what I'm about to do, and neither are surprised. They consider it normal. Perhaps they don't understand it as well as they should, but both have been ordered to stay away from me for at least three months.

In keeping with that advice, Usain is careful to never let me out of his sight. The Hand, carefully laid in its plush, luxurious box, is procured from its comfortable sleeping position and laid out before us. At the same time, The Eye inside its comfortable box is placed together in another magic chamber, an invisible and almost undetectable condition screened behind my brother's Limited Wish.

We stare at The Hand and remark about the lack of any communication attempt emanating from it. This felt as though the artifact was content with its expectations.

"I understand you managed to stand beside Raulston at this moment, and throughout this entire process, doing nothing but watching," Usain realized.

"It was an important learning experience that shall now be passed unto you. This time there will be no crazed running around like a berserker. There is no slamming doors and cupboards open and shut, looking for who-knows-what. I will employ an Alter Reality beforehand to simultaneously invoke the command and make the transition much less painful, less dramatic, and you should use a Limited Wish in the same way. The only device I will need is right here on the table beside me. This handsaw is about to be bestowed with a new name. Handsaw and hand-sawing as things now refer to the sawing of the hand rather than the act of sawing by hand. I find the distinction remarkable and ironic. Also note this is the exact same saw that Raulston employed. I made a point to keep it as a souvenir and will use it again today," I explained.

"I see you saved the blade he used to carve out his head for The Eye. Is that for me?" Usain wondered.

"That is your choice. I don't expect it will make any difference. For me, it's purely sentimental," I said.

"I have always marveled at your melodramatic sentimentality, my dear brother," confessed Usain. "It truly becomes you, and Mother is so proud whenever she hears it."

"And I marvel at the depth of your sarcasm, my dear brother. These traits are destined to serve us well in our decision-making skills going forward. Life permanently changes starting today and I is ready," I declared, and it was accepted.

The Hand lay there, all by itself on the table, just out of reach of my temptation. I'm satisfied with that condition for the moment because, as you may remember, and it is important to emphasize this point, that The Eye is buried behind a Limited Wish. We barred it from invading our thoughts, a situation that would otherwise be unbearable to both of us. We shudder to think what would happen if one of us were suddenly stung by a bad dice roll.

The Hand just lay there in the most benign state I have ever noted. It senses my level of experience and intellect, that I know. It might even recognize me from the Raulston Experiment. On that I can only guess. There is a tendency to procrastinate on these matters, so we have agreed to stick to the schedule and give each other the boot whenever one of us slacks off. We will continue to work together and follow up with The Eye in six or twelve months.

From this moment on my actions are driven by a dream. I grab the harmless handsaw with a fervor that would have most of the multifarious population very worried about what might happen next, not so much for me but for society as a whole. I think it's just time to get on with this and cannot be bothered by public opinion.

With the saw lined up neatly perpendicular so my wrist, I begin to sever into what right away becomes a disgusting, bloody mess. Blood and torn flesh sputters all over the table and floor, and soon a splurge of mulched bone accompanies that. The smell is so special that it deserves a mention as well.

But none of that concerns me. I can only marvel at how quickly the process finishes, and what would normally feel like an excruciating eternity was reduced to a few short moments. The hand attached itself to my boney right stump calmly and completely, and thanks to the Alter Reality, all anticipated discomfort was utterly avoided. Usain was impressed and applauded a job well done.

Let's pause for a moment and acknowledge the improbabilities of this process. I feel a pressing need to impart upon you an analysis of the deeper meaning here. As I said, the indefensible discomfort that we witnessed in Raulston, and that I experienced during my lich transformation, was completely absent this time. There is more to this than the Alter Reality alone would suggest. The spell has had an unexpected effect. The Hand knows. The Hand is in the know. It has waited patiently and conducted itself with resignation and poise, its ego long ago establishing who I am and what I stand for. The Hand has wanted me all along.

What Is Happening With My Gestation Period?

One should have prepared for a long and arduous transformation. I am exempt. Two months of time is invested sitting around contemplating. Usain watches over me, sitting quietly beside me on the messy, rancid floor of our beloved RILF. Nothing has been cleaned since Lorelei was last here. I have already built the necessary rapport with my equal twin, and I do not mean Usain this time. It might come to pass, and I prefer not to mention it out loud just yet, but the green light for Usain to plunge into The Eye could materialize sooner than anticipated. My concern at the moment, and this is only a fleeting whim I get from time to time, is whether The Hand might try to coerce me toward The Eye. As long as The Eye is hidden by our magic, it is safe for moment, but The Hand realizes I know more than I say. The Hand regularly drops subtle hints of inquiry.

Leaving a hand written message for Usain causes a painful flinch in my neck that concerns me deeply. I cannot hide from my own thoughts. The Hand wants to be involved in everything, no matter how insignificant or benign. Because of this, communication with Brother has become risky, especially when speaking out of turn. We have to choose our words.

I now conclude it is necessary for Usain to work through his transition alone. The Hand and The Eye will seek to manipulate us, possibly cause us to make decisions we would later regret. Once Usain's process begins with The Eye, we will be irrevocably bound to each other, but if we are apart, he and I will have better individual control. We might otherwise go totally beserk, rushing into madness until one of us is dead.

"Where do we go from here, Bro," Usain asked, trying not to seem impatient or brash.

He has been patient, I must concede, and forcing him to sit on his hands for another two or three months could be the cause of a new problem. "Are you thinking what I'm thinking?"

"Yes, I've been thinking it non-stop while watching you get settled in. I am envious," Usain reported.

"I'm concerned that we must accept a separation for a while. I don't think it is wise to be together until after completion. You have been remarkably resilient throughout my transition and I am grateful. Unfortunately, I cannot return with an equal gesture in kind. Without verbalizing, you may nod your head in agreement or not. Try your utmost to stay here, safe inside the RILF. I shall return in two months. A clear signal that you comprehend the extreme danger of doing this together a second time is all I need," I explained.

"I understand and accept," Usain declared, and with that prerequisite agreement established, we part ways with my farewell.

A visit to Ersa Calamy is first up. Catching up with Lori and Layla is highest priority. My straight hair has grown longer and has turned completely white. My charisma has changed, mostly in the evaluation of confidence and persuasion, and even through the Font Scry, Layla exudes a level of reverence and awe not discernible before. I will remain mildly skeptical about Goradeya for now, just to be cautious.

The Sisters are completely on side, and with that satisfactory conclusion, I hereby eliminate my biggest worry. I don't know whether they like me more, but my first thorough tailbone licking in ages suggests general improvements. Some bones have proliferated, and upgrades in prestige and pre-eminence offer more nice places to attach sparkling decorations. Lori is fixated on a particular bone, a conspicuous third appendage of a proportion appropriate to my gigantic new right hand. I maintain this is a fine allegory, at least for me.

"No wonder The Hand went to your right! A lefty would certainly have been inconvenient, dear Brother," Lori mused as she set herself into the diligent polishing routine. She attached a sparkly to my bone.

"Let's keep on eye on Usain," I suggested, and in moments the Scrying Font opened sight into the RILF, far to the north from here.

Checking up on our brother is becoming a daily habit. Usain has been in a confusing state of illness and discomfort, some days screaming in terror, other days laughing hysterically. After a month, he had not even attempted The Eye. We see it lying on the table just as it was when I left. Usain was often beside himself, upset, angered, crazy, probably deep in conversation with someone below. Is it through The Eye or does he have something else cooking I'm unaware of?

After seven weeks he took the plunge as expected. Lorelei and I did not witness it first hand, but with the RILF interior totally covered in blood, splattered brain parts all about, and slimy hand prints here and there, it reminded me of the happy times I had with Raulston's book many years ago.

The first several weeks after Usain manually gouged his eye out were not pretty. Using a mallet and a rusty steel flower planting tool, he was unapproachable. Some days he was not inside and this had us deeply worried. On the following days we generally find him sleeping inside, and although the RILF was in a most dire condition, we were always happy to see him return.

"I'll need to Consecrate that house of yours. It's in sad condition," Lori advised.

"I'm going up to see him. I promised to return in two months and that is overdue. We're already into 695 and there's so much unfinished work. Many things at The Peninsula of Hate are falling between the cracks because Usain is indisposed," I lamented, frustrated with having no clue about what to do there. I guess that means I'm a delegating boss.

The Hand has bestowed upon me a broad range of powers, a few benign curses and a couple of serious issues. I can employ a Ball of Fire, Fire Wall, Bolt of Lightning, Cone of Ice, Falling Feather, Dimension Portal and Magic Dispel at my level, each twice a day. I can Monster Fascinate, Person Fascinate and Monster Speak, each usable once a day. The big powers include Gate a Demon, Daemon or Devil Lord once a month. I can Teleport twice a day and Cell Adjust through increased psionic activity, and I have 75% resistance to magic for ten minutes a day. Ulrich and I can communicate over any distance, any removed plane. There are many other minor advantages that I will eventually get around to.

The negatives present concerns. One is an explosion resulting from each use of any prime power is likely to injure me. The bigger problem is a 5% risk of losing intelligence, wisdom and charisma each time a prime power is used. You already know about the white hair and the enlarged bone.

But the one horrifying side effect is the feature I love. It is the most terrible and the most evil magic I have yet come across. I can turn a warm blooded creature into an undead wight by touch. I knew this was coming, watching Raulston work in Kangas. I want this and plan to use such power to great effect. Ulrich should become self-aware of this skill. I am Ulmaetor.

We Go Adventuring

"Best not come near me!" Usain hissed when I appeared inside the RILF. A full ten weeks have passed since I left Usain alone.

"No Usain, look!" I said as I showed him my Hand.

The Hand is huge, ominous looking, and burned black, as though its original creator had been standing in a firey cavern at the time the enchantment was first employed. Ulrich looks good with The Eye properly seated in place, and he no longer appears to suffer. But there does seem to be an unpleasant smell all around, and I wonder some of it might be originating from him.

"What powers have you acquired? Can you create an undead wight by touch?" I asked, eager to know all of what he's experiencing.

"Not a wight, but a shadow! And there is a small percentage for each shadow to develop into a spectre over time! I can Cause Disease by touch, Regenerate and Heal all wounds within six hours, have Fear Immunity and the best part is a double duration Time Stoppage with a ten-foot radius. That's two full minutes in a Time Stoppage for all of us inside its area. That will be kind of useful! Now I can carry a Wish and a Meteor Swarm as daily, standards" exclaimed Ulrich in delight. He is happy.

"Let's go set Fered Soudron on fire!" I burst out, much to Ulrich's satisfaction.

"Let's do that," he agreed.

Teleporting directly into the generally upbeat busy and happy Fered Soudron, our immediate actions include unloading six Balls of Fire and six Fire Walls into the busiest market area. Two Meteor Swarms are sent toward the prominent City Hall and in no time at all large areas of central Fered Soudron are on fire. Innocents by the hundreds are burned or mutilated. Survivors run in panic in all directions and city officials are completely at a loss for solutions. A great strategy is sending Balls of Fire to two major Fire Stations and hampering their ability to respond. All this causes several sections of central Fered Soudron to begin burning out of control, and the dense housing constructed of wood allows many neighborhoods to disappear, reducing themselves into heaps of smoking ash.

Back home to the RILF we return, and by late afternoon the next day we are prepared to repeat the process with another wave. Many of yesterday's fires had not yet been brought under control, much less extinguished, and that allowed us the luxury of selecting specific targets for our next round of fire-based attacks. I doubt we have ever had anywhere near this much fun in all our lives, and the initiative is all our own. We elect to do it again a third day and again on a fourth day, but like anything overdone, by the fifth day there comes a point when such repetition becomes monotonous. Fered Soudron is on its knees. Economic activity is at a stand-still. Some three thousand have been killed and twenty thousand refugees have packed up and fled to Milan. Oh, won't that be interesting!

Chapter 21 : Four Boys Four Girls Three Daemons and Me

Three Newcomers Arrive At Last

With remarkable enthusiasm, Lorelei visits for the Consecration of our beloved RILF. The exuberance wears off pretty quickly when she sees it, and worries that any generous devotion to the task of cleaning up here has no hope. I argue it's the pessimism that diminishes the chance of success, and with that remark, she sets herself into the task with a fervor not ever readily apparent before.

I love Lorelei. It took me a long time to warm up to her, to get used to her, and to accept her, even when she had early on warmed straight to me. The experience with Layla has been precisely the opposite, especially concerning Usain as you know, but while being fully cognizant of all our loyalties and capabilities, she has found her own unique path to greatness. Her relationship with the Arcanadaemon has been as fruitful as we could have hoped for, and our establishment of Gehenna 2 is an unexpected advantage, a satisfactory condition I am grateful for. Perhaps Goradeya is frightened by Usain, and that is wise, because Ulrich is destined to be much, much worse. None of that matters. Each of us has a proprietary tack, and there is a minimum of overlap without redundancy. We are making a dream team, and I am its boss.

As we study, experiment and learn, living in Lori's comfort some days and in the privacy of RILF on others, the year 696 is upon us with surprising immediacy. Usain is now fully complete in the metamorphosis to Ulrich, as though he weren't already, and I have sat on my hands with patience watching his slow and sometimes painful transfiguration materialize. Mine was so much less dramatic. Maybe I was better prepared.

Ulrich presents something big to what is now properly called Team Hades Ulmaetor. It is that great set of assets mentioned previously. We have the fruits of diligent efforts combined with the advantages of his connections on Hades. I must remark on this with interest, because we know Gehenna and Tarterus could not possibly have afforded him such advantages. The opposite is more likely. Without thinking too deeply on it for the time being, we may remember that when Roxanne Gated Usain into our world, we assumed he had come from the same place as the Daerghodaemons, but I now know that cannot have been the case. He had come directly from the Kingdom of Hades. A senior vassal to The Dark Lord himself took Usain under his arm, not in pity, but in mentorship, just as Raulston had done with me. We were both noticed. Usain was being groomed for great darkness, and greatness he will achieve, provided that it corresponds to my objectives. My tremendous rise to leadership was not foreseen, especially since my privately chosen path to Darkness was unprogrammed and unexpected.

The good news does not end quickly. Another big win is in the making, and although none of it is a complete surprise, it amounts to more than I had forecasted. Ulf, Udo and Uriah are mature and ready to join Team Hades Ulmaetor. These fresh liches were presented to Ulrich by The Dark Lord himself, leaving all specialized training and indoctrination entirely to Ulrich's whims. On this point, I found myself faced with a concern. I don't appreciate having to relinquish all control and was never presented with an option. I must confess that, even though there is no reason to doubt my brother or anyone else immediately associated with me, there is an opportunity for infidelity to emerge. Perhaps it is a test of loyalty designed for me to monitor, and if so, I am sensible to the gesture from below. Anyway, in the worst case scenario, I can always pull the plug with violence. Having considered all, I will let myself be content to watch and see how this all plays out.

Ulf, Udo and Uriah are wizards with substantial intelligence and magic capabilities. What's more, all three learned the same base spell list from one school of thought, and so anything new taught by Ulrich to one member is automatically extended to all three. They will reside at The Peninsula, making themselves at home however they choose, but only one of four words is needed to command them into service, one for each or one for all.

It's official. Team Hades Roxanne must now be my primary rival, and I couldn't have picked a better one. Those pathetic bureaucrats surrounding the Athena, Apollo and Aphrodite pantheons need something to keep themselves amused because life over there must seem utterly irrelevant otherwise. They all start with an "A" because half of them couldn't recite the alphabet of the common tongue backwards if their fucking lives depended on it. They're wimps and shouldn't masquerade as anything more than a minor obstacle.

Roxanne had no doubt never expected the outcome placed before her, and although she's lost some face, some followers and a whole bunch of respect, she enjoys the intrigue and will happily engage any challenge we might muster up. She is tough and it is clear that both of us are here to stay. And as predicted, The Dark Lord is watching all the drama with great interest.

Through the marriage pact between Layla and the Arcanadaemon Goradeya, Team Hades Ulmaetor has managed a degree of dominion over Gehenna 2. This has been an unexpected surprise nobody could have foreseen. I must congratulate Ulrich on his behavior when we were there, for his bold initiative was the deciding factor.

"I pledge allegiance to you all and welcome whatever orders I may be given," Ulf energetically stated.

Ulf spoke with a remarkably clear, baritone voice that seemed to occupy a large amount of dimensional space, kind of like a Telempathic Projection.

Ulf, Udo and Uriah all stood side by side, facing Lorelei, Ulrich and I, outside in the Hallucinatory Terrain of Cirsalsomere, the front and back yard of our RILF. Lorelei was moved to be considered Ulf's superior, a point that none of us had given any consideration to until he mentioned it. Team Hades builds itself and there is obviously no need for me to be too formal. The boys are falling neatly in line and appear to have an extra dose of respect for the cleric. Oh, Layla is going to love that!

"I pledge to follow each of you unto death," Udo declared with pride.

"That's good to know, thank you. But Udo - you are already technically dead, aren't you?" Ulrich mused with his scratchy, raspy voice.

"I'm already dead! Then I cannot possibly disappoint you, my Lord Ulrich!" Udo stated with a solid display of humor and humility.

We all had a good laugh. That is funny. Udo's voice is a lighter version of Ulrich's annoying, sand-papery rasp. Let's hope they take all their future arguments well out of ear shot. Nobody will want to hear that.

"I pledge to carry out all orders to their fullest. I will rend, and squeeze, and destroy anything that stands in your way, my Lord Ulmaetor, my Lord Ulrich, my Lady Lorelei" Uriah proclaimed.

Trust the little guy to scream the loudest. That is fairly typical. Lorelei and Ulrich applauded in jest, noting how Uriah's softer, feminine voice encourages him to speak boldly. Lorelei beamed with delight at the new honorific presented to her.

"My goodness, what a honeyed accolade! Did you hear that Ulmaetor, Ulrich? 'Lady' Lorelei! Don't you forget it!" Lori joked with emphasis on the title, and another good laugh was passed around.

She deserves a little leverage and the three boys' first visit to her Ersa Calamy establishment gave her plenty.

Two New Acolytes For Layla and Lorelei

The inaugural group objectives include one or more trips to Gehenna. Procedure has been agreed upon through our regularly scheduled Font Scry and Layla shows up at Lori's the next day. We remark about her altered posture, caused by the heavy, off-center gravity prevalent on her home plane. She dances around on one leg for a while to try and balance it off.

"I will start making weekly trips to this plane. The gravity down there is about to have permanent effects on my body. My poor bones were never designed that way!" moaned Layla, rubbing her knees and waist in frustration.

"I'll come up with something to help with that. If we can postpone our visit there by one day, I'll have a beautiful and permanent solution to those gravity-induced weight and joint problems," offered Ulrich proudly, eager to provide any perk that stands to improve his relationship with her.

"Usain, you are amazing. I will gladly accept whatever you might come up with. Now I have something big to present as well, and if I may suggest postponing the visit to my home by a few additional days, we might experience this other big thing," Layla said with enthusiasm.

The next day, not long after Ulrich completed his Limited Wish, two young girls arrive at Lori's Temple. They did not wait to be invited inside. They did not expect immediate acknowledgement by anyone in particular. They just simply walked in. But one person had long expected them.

"Ulmaetor, Lorelei - let me introduce Lydia and Livia, twin sisters from right here in Ersa Calamy. They are twelve years old and have gravitated toward us for some time. I felt their presence two years ago, and from quite nearby, too. I imagined Lorelei and I would mentor one each," Layla explained.

"Hi," said Lydia softly.

"Hi," added Livia in a similarly girlish tone.

"Well, hello. Welcome to my - our Sanctuary. You are very fortunate to catch all of us together like this," Lorelei said.

"We've been watching two and three times a day for months, hoping for some uptick in activity here. You folks are not often available, so Livia and I decided to more or less camp out on your doorstep," Lydia confessed.

"We are glad for your efforts. And we are rarely here these days, it's true. How do you feel about plane travel?" Layla joked, but I know it wasn't a joke at all.

There is a dilemma on the horizon. How do the girls take on the acolytes they so desperately need while continuing to forge ahead with our busy schedule? Send them to Gehenna, of course! Where else can they get that level of training? That's easier said than done and we'll want to proceed with caution, I suppose.

Layla decides to take Ulrich down with her. I am so gratified watching how she has warmed to him. The connection between them is complex and goes infinitely deep. A permanent rift there cannot be tolerated. There can only be negative consequences that my enemies will exploit, especially that cock-licking bitch up the street. But never to have uttered a single stern word of warning is hugely satisfactory to me. It has made my life so much easier and I love watching the relationship repair all on its own. Ulrich is beaming from ear to ear at the invitation and is more than happy to go.

The Limited Wish proves to settle all the issues Layla has listed and extends to Goradeya when he visits us. Yes, it's true. Layla plans to bring her husband on an occasional trip up here, and tomorrow will be the first. Escorting an Arcanadaemon to Ersa Calamy should be quite the news story for the local tabloid.

The Gehenna Crew

For some while going forward, I'm going to let those present stand in my place to tell the story of the journey as it happens. I am not there. I decide to stay behind at Lori's to play Papa. Lori and I need to massage this acolyte thing.

"I really like it here," Ulrich noted again, realizing its familiarity from his earliest years here and on The Planes of Hades.

"Would you like to trade places? I don't think Goradeya would mind either way! Still, I must congratulate you on your Herculean magic, Ulrich. It is truly mind-blowing. I feel so much more comfortable now. Gravity is straight down, just as it should be and seems thirty percent less," stated Layla.

"Are we bringing Goradeya back with us? I wonder he would not appreciate the Prime Material plane too much were it not for my magic alterations," Ulrich mused.

"Yes, and I have another earth-shaking surprise to unleash. Do you remember Boshnash the Skin Ripper and Filcher the Bone Crusher? Those two dunderheads are extremely afraid of Roxanne as you know. Fun for us is they haven't suffered me yet! I can do whatever I want; Goradeya won't mind! Just watch! Also Ulrich, there is another important point to note. You know the Daemons jitter with nervousness and apprehension hearing your name mentioned - all of them - because of what you did to Goradeya's incestuous twin. There isn't a Daemon anywhere, nowhere in all of the Neutral Evil underworld, that hasn't gossiped the names Ulrich and Roxanne. And they have no idea what you look like. I hope to be the third name on the list quite soon! Roxanne was my mentor and I picked up a trick or two, and am now ready to let them rip," Layla slowly explained, savoring every word with delicious detail.

"I am looking forward to the show, and I will be ready with the unimaginable should it for whatever reason be deemed necessary," Ulrich promised.

"Ulrich, I want to apologize for how badly I treated you earlier on. I was wrong and I'm sorry. I misunderstood many things, and mostly I misunderstood who you really were and what your destiny was to be. When I recognized how much you admired and cherished Mother - and when I zoned in on your unconditional loyalty to your brother, our brother, our leader - I knew my judgement had to be amiss," Layla explained in what surely was genuine penitence and sorrow.

"Thank you my dear, beautiful sister. Don't trouble yourself another minute about it. I loved you, anyway. I have loved you and Lorelei the moment I learned of your existence. I was so excited. Mother had two daughters. That was just beyond amazing to me. And you are both so beautiful and talented. One day I'll tell you about my early life growing up as a crippled boy in Kangas, together with Ulmer. There are many things even he would never learn. Nobody ever treated me with the barest minimum of respect. I have always been the runt, the mutt - the whipping boy that everyone used for their convenience - their patsy and their scapegoat, and I was physically unable to defend myself from every finger pointed at me for whatever stupid reason. That was my curse from Day One. That was Proctor and Paulina's curse. But, that was also my role, I knew. I'm used to it," lamented Ulrich, delivering all details with surprising candor and sincerity.

"It was prerequisite in forging who you are today, I suspect. Nobody has earned their status like brothers Ulmaetor and Ulrich," judged Layla with the new, deeply seated admiration.

No other words were said about it as Layla and Ulrich approached the dark, shadowy palace of the Arcanadaemon, Layla's home. The towering black, steel fence looked like a row of shining pikes and spears all neatly lined up, ready to defend. Perhaps that is what they are. The poor visibility in this dark, gloomy atmosphere would not permit any straightforward attack, and the high ground onto which the palace was perched afforded another useful defense.

"Goradeya Sire, shall we summon the two Daerghodaemons?" Layla asked.

"Yes my Lady, in fact they are already here. I expect they will be pleased to see you both," Goradeya politely stated.

Stepping into another massive chamber complete with an obsidian tile floor and black columns throughout, the Daerghos had been busy wrestling, and the room thus presented us with a most disagreeable body odor. The Daerghos have a certain smell, and not a very pleasant one.

"Filcher and Boshnash! I see you are both well! Why do you smell so bad? It is absolutely fucking rank in here!" Layla complained.

Layla pretended to be annoyed and that set the desired tone straight off. The two meatheads were quite bewildered and unable to think well, not that they ever could. Their five arms and three legs flailing randomly about never fail to make a humorous spectacle.

"Oh Layla! We are so sorry. We didn't know you were here. Say, let us clean this place up. We'll make it all nice again, okay? Oh Layla, who is your companion today? We haven't had the pleasure of being introduced," Boshnash waffled and whined, sounding all agitated and nervous.

"Yeah, who's your friend? He looks like a great guy. We wanna be friends, too," Filcher eagerly stated.

"Boshnash, Filcher - I'd like you to meet my brother Ulrich," Layla said.

"Oh, hello Ulrich. Oh wait a minute - Ulrich? Oh, you don't mean THAT Ulrich, do you? This is your brother Ulrich, right," Boshnash reasoned.

"This is my brother Ulrich, yes that's correct. He is indeed also that Ulrich you have gossiped so much about," Layla said, smiling brightly.

"Oh, that Ulrich! Your brother! Oh, no! Oh, no! We had no idea you had a brother named Ulrich," Filcher whined as he wrapped his limited mind around the concept of a sibling relationship, one involving an already infamous Ulrich.

By now, Boshnash had also begun to accept the truth, and both of them started dancing aimlessly about, bumping into each other, adding even more to the profuse smell. Their heads spun round and round, axes perched high on their necks, and in opposite rotation to one another. Dizzy and disoriented, they nearly knocked each other over several times.

"Come on now, you jelly-headed morons, settle down. We have tons of work to do!" advised Layla.

"Work? Layla, sweet, kind Lady! What work?" asked Filcher in despair.

"You two muttonheads will accompany us to the Prime Material, to Ersa Calamy. Won't that be fun?" joked Layla to the dynamic duo.

"Oh yes, but that's where Roxanne lives! Oh, please please, sweet kind Lady Layla, don't take us to Roxanne's! She isn't kind to us at all!" Boshnash pleaded.

"Don't worry, Boshnash. We aren't going to see Roxanne. However, you'll soon discover I have acquired many of Roxanne's skills, all the ones that scare the shit out of you boys, too. And just to be clear, this brother of mine here, this Ulrich? Ulrich is a popular name now, but he is indeed THAT Ulrich, so no funny business, okay boys?" Layla suggested.

"We gotcha! No funny business, no Lady Layla. Definitely! No," both zipperheads agreed.

Plane Shifting up to the Prime Material went smoothly with the use of The Wand of The Planes. It is one of many things she inherited from Deyagora's assassination. Apparently he had used it regularly to travel between Gehenna and Hades, and occasionally even Tarterus whenever he was stuck in the mood for a sunny vacation.

Livia and Lydia are as bright-eyed as I have seen anyone get, but they are not afraid. Lydia laughs out loud at the Daerghos' spinning heads, thinking they must be some kind of comedy freak show, a popular theater attraction in Ersa Calamy these days. Boshnash and Filcher are indeed a comedy freak show, whether they might wish it so or not, and if they don't prove their worth as soldiers, it is good to know another occupation exists for them right here.

"Boys, when you want to go back home, just let me know! I can send you down instantly with the Unholy Utterance! You might have sore ears and a headache, so I can always take you down the manual way if you prefer," Layla clarified, trying not to burst out laughing throughout the explanation.

All twelve of us were together for the first time, and it will eventually prove to be the only time to be together on The Prime Material. Procedure and formality present an imbalance of organizational idiosyncrasies I have little patience for, and the Gehenna crew really never enjoy making the ascension for any reason, so why bother pushing it. Future meetings therefore compel us to go down there, and Goradeya very much appreciates our resolve to make it so. Usain is happy to go for whatever reason and Layla is under no pressure to make any changes to her domestic circumstances. The Daerghos were just beginning to enjoy all the attention they were getting in Ersa Calamy and were sad to leave so soon, but quickly realized their time had come.

Lorelei decides to make time for Lydia and Livia's parents. Having the girls intern at "The Temple Down The Street" doesn't seem like much of a hassle, but spending the next two years of their childhood lives on Gehenna 2 might require guardian approval. And with all that solved, I get another idea.

Chapter 22 : Fered Loron

Fered Loron - A Description

"Oh, beautiful Fered Loron! Let's visit there on our next holiday!" everyone everywhere is heard saying.

The tourist brochures are full of enthusiasm, and so full of it. Whether it's The Stone City of Steps, or The Step City of Stone, or The City of Stones and Steps, nobody is ever quite sure. What an extraordinary village, with its 1800 residents, purposefully supported on a solid rock foundation, by no means level, steeply inclined against its stark, metamorphic mountainside.

Elevation at its single entrance gate below is already at 3500 feet. Sheer cliffs drop on all sides, contrasting against the abrupt, vertical face of the mountainside against the town's back, at its 4400-foot elevation a perfect location for a Hades Temple, the highest possible landing in the city. Here the beginnings of a depleted atmosphere is the limit that soldiers can tolerate, but it doesn't bother me. This landing ramps squarely against the vertical rise, climbing up to the 1-mile high summit, providing a view so grand as to make the mightiest of mountain dwelling dragons envious. But then who cares about stupid dragons and how they feel.

Relatively low, 25-foot ramparts with sentry stations along the lower town area, form a U-shape leaning against the rugged, towering hillside, and the narrow, winding road leading up to the village gates requires a considerable expenditure of effort and courage just to traverse. No settlement is more impervious to an attack than Fered Loron, and considering the severe limitations of physical space leading up to the town's front gate, even a short siege would soon demoralize the perpetrators.

The view over the expansive, fertile lowlands of Sodon Sovany is unhampered by any additional obstructions, by virtue of this being the southernmost peak in the range, and the sentry guards' main challenge is keeping themselves from drifting away into a peaceful snooze while on duty each day. They ought to have something a little more reliable attached to this duty, but before I arrived no meaningful form of organized aggression had ever taken place here.

Fered Loron's larger concerns are the ongoing negotiations with Mother Nature. Meteorological phenomena such as avalanches, violent storms and water deluges take place with dependable frequency. Geological mishaps like earthquakes and rock slides keep everyone vigilant. The prospect of boulders dropping out of nowhere and without warning, crashing down in the town square at night, is especially entertaining during evening festivities outside. Boulders smash through residential rooftops at all hours. These events cause considerable confusion, not to mention damage, and an emergency response team should at some point be put in place to deal with all of that.

I get another crackhead idea that compels me to spiral further downhill. I'm going to enslave Fered Loron, and maybe obliterate it from the map, depending on the final analysis. Total annihilation seems just about right. While it has proven impervious to any sort of conventional assault, for us it will be such an easy win. There is no defense against the likes of Team Ulmaetor.

This isn't a job for the clerics. In fact, even considering my pledge to keep the girls in the loop, I elect not to tell them anything about the nutjob idea I am currently occupied with. They'll suspect all kinds of crazy things, and since it isn't easy for me to keep anything secret from them for long, I drop a few early hints to speed up the process. They can go right ahead and Deity Commune the rest of it.

Ulrich, Ulf, Udo, Uriah and I experiment with Teleportation and Shadow Walking to get to The Step City of Stone and perpetrate its demise. We completely circumvent the need to trudge up the dangerous path leading to the entrance. Nevertheless, the town presents its list of additional military challenges. By virtue if its steep incline against the mountainside, we immediately recognize how rolling rocks released from above can effectively be deployed to combat an attack from below. Never fight uphill, they say, unless you're in a spot without a better option. In that case, you go in screaming as loud as you can and intimidate the shit out of your adversary.

Ulrich's Eye, the way I prefer to refer to it now, has indeed given him one ability common to both Artifacts: a command word and a touch from either of us creates an undead out of a warm-blooded mammalian life form. This can be a zombie, ghoul, shadow, ghast, wight or wraith, depending on our mood, but an additional expenditure of effort is required for the creation of the wraith form. The others are easy, so it usually makes sense to maximize the wight count whenever possible.

However, given the prevailing geological constraints, focusing on undead entities lacking corporeal substance seems wise, and we elect to weigh in on the creation of shadows for the population at large and wraiths for the gifted minority. We soon learn there is a ten percent chance of a wraith to emerge as a specter, and while the expenditure of effort to produce one is extremely large, the payback is astonishing. The specter is a born leader and will gladly help us get the job done.

It takes a mere three days and three nights to give the population a complete going over. Daylight proves advantageous for the five of us. The limited undead activity in the daytime instills a false sense of security. Some thirty percent manage to hide themselves successfully, but they discover that simply surviving in a situation so miserable does not constitute a win. It is downright horrible. Half of the survivors soon succumb through misplaced trust and bad judgement, especially at night, and when the smoke finally clears, only three hundred of the former residents remain unscathed.

The weather is as perfect as any tourist could hope for, a rare bonus affixing its stamp and seal on this auspicious day. It is so gratifying to be employed here, on a beautiful day such as this. The streets are spotless and completely deserted, and the long shadows produced by the gorgeous directional sunlight make for a perfect postcard painting. Occasionally someone can be seen darting between buildings, screaming in terror, a mishap jaggedly incongruous with the overall mood of this otherworldly setting.

I am unsure what else I can say to make you better appreciate the perfection accomplished here. What other grotesque detail may I impart upon you that stamps an irrevocable impression on your mind that is not already there? It really isn't so much the details of this accomplishment that matter. What matters is the retaliation I anticipate in response.

The Great Council Is Compelled To Respond

I can feel it all around me. The GCV has taken notice. We can sense the barrage of magic all about, picking and probing here and there, following our every move and thwarting our advances. I think it is far too little too late, honestly speaking, for the bulk of the work is already behind us and done. But we will be engaged in another kind of adventure shortly.

It is time to solicit the help of Lorelei, Layla and Goradeya, and they are with us in Ersa Calamy within a day. Perhaps they do not appreciate being left out of all the fun but should nevertheless make themselves ready to conjoin with the midstream conditions I have available.

Returning to the RILF in Cirsalsomere lets us experience the full package. The Great Council of Victory has not only found our refuge, they have dispelled all our hallucinations and killed all the trolls and gnolls still bumbling about in confusion. To make matters worse, they have hacked RILF and made it disappear. This presents a significant concern because Ulrich and I have long been keeping field copies of our spell books inside. Now these are not our backup library nor our traveling books, but several weeks of work will be required to replace them if lost or destroyed.

Sandon the Wise and King Falin, Lord of Tarnash-Gindy's Land of The Far Eastern Dwarves, wherever the fuck that is, are present representing the schmuck Zeus, the Über-God who keeps acting like the dude in charge. Father Elitch, Joey and Lord Aisodon, or Icabod, are here backed by Athena, whatever good that will do. Marshall Kesselring and St. Bodan are present representing Apollo, and Genoivieve is here all by her poor little lonesome, bringing up the rear for Aphrodite, like as though any of it will make any difference.

What immediately strikes me, and I must pause for a moment, calm down, take a breath and contemplate all this in depth, is the startling appearance of Genoivieve. She is, if you'll allow me to boldly admit, a stupendously beautiful creature I had not been adequately prepared for. A princess of her caliber does not seem to fit into in this friggin' bung hole of a situation we have created here, but here she is nevertheless, ready to place a disadvantage on any weak-minded soul in attendance before her. Our fortune is that we have no soul.

Layla is beautiful too, but her style of beauty might best be described with specific embellishments. A caveat here and there is needed, depending on your flavor. But Genoivieve is an exquisite magnificence, a heart-stopping decoration no artist could do justice to.

An obvious wall of jealousy gets thrown up, and I see how Layla and Genoivieve immediately zero in onto each other like cobalt magnets to nickel-plated steel. I'm on pins and needles with anticipation now, wondering whether and when something fun is about to happen here, but let's stop and accept that the difference between their rank and position is zero, and a show here would constitute the fairest of fights if ever there were one.

"What are you looking at, you disgusting mangy dog," uttered Layla first, not loudly so everyone would hear, but in a full mockery directed at Genoivieve.

"Tramp has some nerve talking to me, stupid Hades whore. Crawl back under your mountain of shit and suck your bone?" Genoivieve responded in haste.

This descends into a vivacious but short exchange. Such verve! Such fun!

"You rancid Aphrodite skank! Squat your south-mouth on a guided cradle and rotate!" Layla barked, describing in detail what I though was a perfectly reasonable response.

"Shag yourself with a rusty pike, you spunk gobbling orc slut," responded Genoivieve kindly.

The very next move comes as another surprise. Genoivieve runs straight toward Layla, unleashing a point-blank Psionic Blast. A non-psionic might question the efficacy of such a daring move, but I'm here to tell you that there are two objectives. Layla's erratic response instantly informs Genoivieve about Layla's psionic capability, and I must admit I had no idea Genoivieve was a powerful psionic until just now. Her Psionic Blast was a prodigious monstrosity. I felt it was strong, even while standing on the sidelines well out of range. The second benefit is Genoivieve gets a detailed picture of Layla's intelligence, and possibly her combined intelligence, wisdom and even charisma attributes. This advises a deeper picture into Layla's overall magic capability and highlights a weakness to exploit.

Layla's unrehearsed response to the attack is not especially good. She suddenly becomes absurdly irritated and irate, descending in character to the point of losing her faculties and her usual steadfast judgement. This instantaneous abatement of her character accelerates the involuntary unleashing of the one and only one Unholy Utterance

Layla possesses. This causes some confusion all around. Everyone is deafened by the blast, but there is another thing to report, a matter that has to go down in the history books as a profound embarrassment.

Layla sent her husband Goradeya back down to his home plane of Gehenna 2 by accident. He was standing right beside her.

This is not likely going to play out well, certainly not into our favor. Ulrich motions to the boys and Layla, Lorelei and I coalesces to each other. A Teleport and a Teleport Recall are all that are needed to meet up at Lorelei's comfortable establishment down south.

"I'm so sorry. I don't know what got into me. I can't understand it," Layla confided, clearly demoralized and frustrated.

I cannot doubt her sincerity. None of it was her fault. The whole thing did not play out as expected and she is understandably embarrassed. It's time to be good boss and give Layla a big hug. She deserves a little down time to get over this.

"Don't worry your pretty little head about it. It wasn't your fault. Genoivieve is a damned monster. I never expected such belligerent resolve from her. None of us did. I guess we should be happy none of the other big names there did anything but stand around and watch. It could have been much worse. The ugliest thing for us is that RILF is gone. That happened well before we arrived. Cirsalsomere is history. And our working spell books have fallen into the hands of that dork Joey, whatever his friggin' stupid real name is. Lori's portable Temple and Scrying Font are gone. The boxes of our Artifacts are gone. I suppose we don't actually need the RILF and we don't need Cirsalsomere anymore," I explained as I held my sister close, hoping she might feel better. I need her functioning in the usual tip top form. This set-back is much less important than she realizes.

"I hate that fucking bitch Genoivieve. How can anything be so beautiful and so ugly at the same time?" complained Layla in disgust.

"Believe me, I'm surprised, too. She is something to consider. That's for sure. One day she will become a gigantic problem, perhaps even a headache for the GCV. That I have now come to realize," I elucidated.

"Come on Ulrich. We'll need to get our noses into it and rewrite the working spell books. I'll get you to do both wizard books because my illusionist tome is going to be a task. Fortunately, my old bedroom here is still set up for that sort of work. Lorelei hasn't touched anything," I advised.

"Who would? I've never seen so many creepy disgusting things in jars. I thought best to just close the door and leave it all in darkness," Lorelei mused.

"That was wise!" I agreed in jest.

"You know what? I wonder maybe that goof Joey won't even be able to read our books. They're so heavily encrypted and the language is unlike anything he probably knows," wondered Ulrich out loud.

"Don't hope too much. Joey is a very resourceful wizard. He is the most storied of Arch-Mages in existence. My dear brother, catch him if ever you can! I augur he'll find a way to decipher our work, and rewrite it and then shelve it by destroying the original books," I predicted.

"What a friggin' waste," Ulrich lamented.

"That it is. Let's get to work. I have a feeling 'a few weeks' are not going to be enough."

Chapter 23 : Fered Calamy

It's Already 699

"I never thought it would take this long," Ulrich said, feeling utterly spent.

"We were wise to give the girls some space. Let's check in and see where they're at. What matters is we're done. Finally!" I remarked in relief.

The loss of our RILF proved more expensive than I had at first proclaimed. That goes down as a lesson: never be too optimistic when so many major risks are present. Keep it realistic. I understand why RILF was as much a bane to our team as a benefit and I now worry that Lorelei's establishment here in Ersa Calamy will also become a target. Who better to expropriate it than Roxanne? She would be immune to all its defenses.

Layla and Lorelei have risen well, both in status and capability. They are well employed by their needs as proponents of the Hades Pantheon. In its due course 699 is upon us, and Layla finds herself on the receiving end of her second dose of the Unholy Utterance. Lori gets good at Healing Injuries and Animation and Barriers and Banquets but The Utterance still manages to remain a mystery. She's mighty eager for The Devil Exaction, that I know. I remember Layla long ago warned her that delays would happen and why being cloistered like that Elitch just makes the passage of time unbearable.

Lorelei has masons come in to engrave a giant white Pentagram and a golden Thaumaturgic Triangle across the new obsidian floor of the Temple. They look great and will prove immensely useful if and when she ever gets noticed by the Boss downstairs and gains access to the top tier spells.

Ulrich and I put our heads deep into the magic. It's perfect for us, because unlike the girls, we are not prone to gain weight from sitting on our lazy asses for extended periods. Anyway, the effort expended in rewriting our craft proved once and for all why spells are our most important foundation, and who better than the top guys to concern themselves with that. I didn't intend to be rhetorical.

The three boys were advised to stay busy bettering themselves working as a team. They elect to live with Layla and Goradeya on Gehenna 2 for a year. They learn much about the workings of the Underworld, and not only on the relatively peaceful Planes of Gehenna. They spend considerable time on the Planes of Tarterus and Pandemonium as well. A crazy story from three eager apprentices is welcome whenever we have a moment to spare, and their enthusiasm is always intoxicating.

But there is a point when all the good news begins to wear thin. Time has flown by and although we have risen and grown in many ways, I worry that our competitors have done better. St. Bodan has managed to enlist a huge driving force for Apollo in Milan, and his first acolyte Burk has become deeply indoctrinated as well. He'll be established in no time I predict. We certainly aren't the first to recognize Layla's new bestie Genoivieve. She is a whole new power center in Aphrodite, a pantheon that hadn't garnered the slightest drop of respect from mortals before she came along. Worse is that cute little kid Ninmeşaora, that six-year-old mouse that prophesied my explosive rise to power, is now the gifted first acolyte to Genoivieve. Those girls have every skilled mercenary with sword in hand scrambling for the chance to stand guard for them.

Over in The Neutral Alliance, Vespertine's acolyte Karim has developed a buddy-buddy pact with the ex-Raulston illusionists Shaman Learus and Fred G Gearbox and the Druids Sir Daniel The

Grand and Kadrah The Hierophant. Karim is also about to be established in Milan, and I hear a rumor The Vortex intends to secure the southern village of Sovan Cunard in his name. Can someone please tell me what the fuck is happening here? I can't fucking look away for five damn minutes and not see the competition ooze in all around. They're asphyxiating us like an industrial chemical spill. Losing our RILF did indeed come with collateral damage.

The Time To Act Is Now

We are bound to do something big, and we would like to start immediately. I've been thinking over that nearby river port Fered Calamy and the juicy opportunity that awaits there. It's right in our own back yard, and nowhere else is there such an obvious redundancy. A year ago would have been better, because now there are those two new Apollo-Aphrodite power centers in Milan we will have to deal with. They will surely rise up in Fered Calamy's defense, though Layla is longing for another chance to whack away at that Genoivieve and even the score. She will happily lick her bones as advised and it will taste so sweet.

With Goradeya preferring to sit this out, the seven of us make a few early reconnaissance visits to Fered Calamy, a bustling village of 2,500, the nearest upriver port directly south of Milan, and the fifth municipality of Sodon Calamy. It remains peaceful, unencumbered and vulnerable, and being geographically situated right in our own neighborhood, nobody will suspect anything bad until it's too late.

Countless river craft actively deployed for fishing, freight and taxi services line up and down along the western bank of the River Sodon, conveniently crowding as near as possible to the gigantic, towering city gates. Despite sentry towers prominently stationed on the city wall ramparts directly above, the gates are not as effective as their designers must have engineered for. When ready, I'll have Ulrich blast them open and leave nothing but splinters. This can be affected through the use of his favorite kind of awesome force, the Swarm of Meteors, the same thing that destroyed Deyagora. The Swarm gets attention and respect like nothing else.

Inside the front gate, we are met with a bustling market spanning several streets running north-south. Turning left here guides you towards an internal wall with another giant door, five meters high and utterly impossible for one person to open. This wall, visibly identical to the perimeter constructions, divides the inner confines of the city center into two distinct burroughs north and south.

Walking straight ahead west from the gates takes you down a wide boulevard that opens up into a circular, tree-lined agora graced with hotels and the elegant homes of the town elite. The Fered Calamy City Hall and adjacent buildings dominate the northwest section of the agora circle.

The thing about Fered Calamy's internal layout that I find interesting is how the town is perfectly divided into two halves, separated by the east-west internal wall with adjoining ramparts above. Sentry towers at the junctions to the perimeter walls permit strategic observation of activities in both north and south burroughs of the town as well as everything going on outside the city. It's curious how the primary residential area was built into the southern burrough, completely separate from the commercial area north, and I am stumped trying to comprehend the mysterious purpose behind this particular architecture.

According to Ulrich's analysis, the giant door connecting the north and south burroughs would be kept shut in times of concern, and an additional level of protection could be afforded to civilians during a crisis. Sad is that this honorable feature will not be serviceable during the our uprising, other than it might prove immensely useful to us in formulating an efficient and effective take-down strategy. They will just trap themselves inside.

On our very next visit, Ulrich lets The Swarm rip point blank, aimed toward the main city gates. Fire Resistances all around from the girls greatly minimize our exposure. The poor gates were utterly obliterated, and I am able to disclose that I would never want to be on the receiving end of that brutality.

Other than the several dozen residents instantly exterminated near the entrance, a good sized fire begins to tear through the market area, a place where too much fuel oil had long been lying about. That killed some more folks before it was put under control. The market was a festering fire hazard that simply hadn't bothered anyone until Ulrich came by, but none of that matters now. They extinguished it pretty quickly.

The advance of fighters on foot and on horses, spurred on by the sounding horns from the rather lethargic sentry guard, is instantly thwarted by my Improved Phantasmal Force, a vision utterly confusing everyone. To the uninitiated, the town now appears in reverse, north is south and east is west. It's beautiful. The girls put up Truths of Sight to stay in the loop, but not before unleashing a tandem of Prayers, skewing both attacks and defenses strongly in our favor.

The Fered Calamy response team is inept. There hasn't ever been an effective response to speak about. A few Magic Missiles and Chains of Lightning wrap most things up early. We Fire Ball the office of the mayor and sentry guard stations and send Bolts of Lightning throughout the admin and guard offices.

A few poorly directed arrows come down from above and in response, one single volley of Magic Missiles from all five wizards is required to end it. By this time, the giant internal door was pulled shut and locked from the South Precinct. Walking on Air and Dimension Portal allow all seven of us easy access to the southern burrough. This is where the vast majority of common residents have hemmed themselves in, confident they are safe.

The dreadful process of ghoul, ghast and wight manufacture commences now, but not before we make an instantaneous return to Ersa Calamy to rest, study and restore our arsenals. It's good to stop and prepare for the next chapter. Day One has been stupendously productive and trouble-free, and we feel cautiously optimistic Day Two will be a genre of comedy. The seven of us, one illusionist, two clerics and five wizards - because I count as two - are a force to contend with. Honestly, I think we must see about getting a fighter among us, but are making do without one, even if it's unsustainable.

Time is of paramount importance and rest is not now wise. We get ourselves straight back to duty before the GCV has a chance to muster, but I guess they aren't awake yet.

The Fered Calamy general population has officially deemed safety can only be guaranteed hiding behind the closed doors of their homes. While I acknowledge the moral superiority of this decision, the sad truth is that our lives have again been made easier. With five wizards in my team Wizard Locking main doors to all high density apartment blocks, we need but one wight per building to initiate the task of transforming all its residents. He'll tell his two friends, and they'll tell their parents, and they'll tell their siblings and so on and so forth. The simplicity of the strategy is both exceedingly sad and exceptionally funny. There just isn't much for us to do. Once the apartment blocks are done, we can let the wights out at night like good doggies. They'll sniff out and chase after all those warm-blooded entities cooped up in the smaller dwellings, starting with their pets. Nobody expects to be attacked by their own loyal dog.

Ghouls appear to have excelled in the northern business burrough while the southern area has almost exclusively been dominated by wights. One aspect of this worth noting is that wights are relatively solitary, and this feature has worked out well among the general population. Ghouls in contrast appear to thrive under conditions of command. Authority is channeled through the slightly more powerful ghasts, and we are witnessing how ghasts have concentrated themselves on assuming the former town elite. Perhaps they aren't as brain dead as we thought. Influence before secures influence today, and the hundred or so rank and file civic employees are falling neatly in line. Civic ghouls they are. The small number of surviving law enforcement personnel become terrifying in their resolve to make Master happy, and the undead domestic animals from homes and farms give new meaning to diversity.

It really is quite the spectacle. Occasionally a survivor wearing nothing but pajamas or underwear darts across the agora screaming, only to be hunted down and eaten by a band of opportunistic ghouls lurking behind the next corner. Someone should have informed them that screaming is most definitely not in their best interest. Silence obviously improves ones chances of survival, but it is a little late to be proselytizing now.

Now and then I see domestic cats appearing from under stairs, endeavoring to collect food. Cats are the perfect hunters, and their efforts to bring in mice or deliciously nutritious insects might certainly help keep the indoor pest populations under control. Ghouls and wights likely do not possess sufficient dexterity to catch these cats, nor mice for that matter, and another survival niche has thus been carved out there.

Now comes the looting we have patiently waited for. It is the reward, that aspect of murder and subjugation that gets Ulf, Udo and Uriah so excited. They haven't yet experienced such pleasure on this level. We make ourselves stupendously rich cashing in on a whole towns wealth. It's easy with the girls employing the Object Location. City Hall and select citizens had over the course of countless decades amassed an enormous fortune in coins and small gems, ostensibly in the form of obligatory taxes, but gifts and bribes also tallying up very well. The bribes prove to be so much easier to carry and let us not worry about leaving behind wagon loads of low denominations.

The GCV will be obligated to come at us, but something now tells me they'll waste time working to right the wrongs we have created. Fered Loron and Fered Calamy urgently need help, and we have made a mess that cannot easily be corrected. Retaliation cannot be the first GCV objective when there are more pressing matters. That would just be evil.

We shall use this money to set up better security for Team Ulmaetor. We will all move to Gehenna 2. Lorelei's Temple in Ersa Calamy can become Lydia and Livia's establishment as soon as they are able to assume that responsibility. The GCV will not harm them because there is no benefit and no value in making juniors pay for the actions of their superiors. Roxanne on the other hand, will always bear watching.

And so that's where it was left. That's when we left. The GCV go on a clean-up mission and leave us alone, at least for now. There will always be a future reckoning, but for today, we have effectively evened the score without confrontation. But now newcomers like Burk and Ninmeşaora and Karim will be given great opportunities to spread their wings, so who really came out ahead do you think? Not Roxanne at least.

APPENDICES

© Martin Werner Zander

APPENDIX I : GLOSSARY of SPELLS CANTRIPS DISCIPLINES and ABBREVIATIONS

[A p-I-1] CANTRIPS

A PHRODITE -
GENOIVIEVE and VANITA's LIST :
Cause Fart / Hiccup / Burp /
Sneeze / Cough
Exterminate Insect
Cause Uncontrollable Urination /
Involuntary Diarrhea
Heal Light Scrapes, Burns and Bruises
Tip Glass Over
Get Ready
Animate Musical Instruments
Animate Copy Write Quill
MESHA and REN's LIST :
Cause Urgent Diarrhea
Do Nails Hair Make-Up and Wash
Change Hair Color
Mosquito Repellent
Create Hot Drink
Grow Flowers and Herbs
Stir Potion Mixture - Duration 1 hour/level

Get Dressed - Change Again
Dust Laundry & Dishes, Iron,
Fold, Wipe & Sweep
Catalog Material Components

APOLLO -
St. BODAN and BURK'S LIST :

Cause Spontaneous Erection
Cause Spontaneous Ejaculation
Cause Spontaneous Urination
Mini Mosquito Swarm
Create Cold Alcoholic Beverage
Create Party Snacks
Open Door
Play Musical Instruments
Copy Write Quill

[Ap-I-2] CLERIC SPELLS

Top Level Powers ⬦
     Second Tier Major Powers ⬦

See also Appendix [Ap-II] : "*The Textbook For Strategic Shock and Awe*" for more cleric spell information, especially for coaching on how certain spells might be interpreted.

Note that many spells and cantrips are reversible even though not specifically labeled as such. In some cases the reverses are more powerful and less expected.

Aerial Attendant ⬦
     Animating the Dead
Animating Objects or Object Animation
Animating Dead Monsters ⬦
Atonement Ceremony
Astral Traveller ⬦
Banquet of Heroes ⬦ or Feast of Heroes
Barrier of Blades ⬦
Blindness Removal
Chanting
Cloud Burst
Cold Resistance
Commanding
Consecrate Ground Ceremony
Continuous Light
Continuous Darkness

Cure Light Injury
Cure Serious Injury
Cure Critical Injury
Curse Removal
Devil Exaction ✧
Deity Commune ✧
Deity Gate ✧
Deity Gate Demon Lord, Arch Devil, Oino
Disease Cure or Disease Cures
Divine Augury
Divine Predictions
Earthquake ✧ Seismic Infusion
Evil Detection
Evil Protection
Evil Protection 10' Radius
Exorcism
Fear Removal
Feast of Heroes ✧ Banquet of Heroes
Feeblemind Removal
Feeblemind
Finding Traps
Finding the Path ✧
Flame Bolt
Fire Resistance
Fire Wall
Forbidding Entry ✧
Glyph
Golem
Harm ✧ (Heal All Injuries in Reverse)
Heal All Injuries ✧
Heat Resistance
Holy Symbol

Invisibility

Know Alignment

Lie Detection or Detect Lie

Life Detection or Detect Living

Light

Lowering Water (Raising Water Reversed)

Magic Dispel

Magic Stone

Meşa's Magnificent Wield ◈

Monster Speak ◈ Speaking Monster

Negative Material Plane Protection

Neutralizing Poisons

Object Animation ◈ or Animating Objects

Object Location

Paralysis Removal

Parting of The Sea ◈

Path Finder ◈

Person Hold

Plague of Insects or Stinger Plague

Plane Shifting ◈

Plant Speak

Pray or Prayers

Quest

Raising Dead ◈

Raising Multiple Dead (Team Apollo) ◈

Raising Water (Lowering Water)

Regeneration ◈

Restoration ◈

Resurrection ◈

Scrying Font or Font Scry

Seismic Infusion ◈ or Earthquake

Silence in a 15' Radius

Slowing Poisons
Speaking With Plants
Speaking With Animals
Speaking With Monsters ◈
Speaking With Stone ◈ Stone Speak
Stinger Plague or Plague of Insects
Sticks and Snakes or Snake Sticks
Succor ◈
Teleport Recall ◈
The Holy Utterance ◈ The Unholy
Tongues
Truth of Sight ◈
Truth of Distance Sight ◈ (Team Apollo)
Walk Like Wind or Walk the Wind ◈
Walking on Air ◈ Air Walking
Walking on Water
Watching Wyverns
Water Parting ◈ Parting the Sea
Weather Control ◈
Weather Control Advanced ◈ (Apollo)

[Ap-I-3] PSIONIC ATTACK and DEFENSE MODES, PSIONIC DISCIPLINES

A TTACK MODES
    Id Insinuator
Psionic Blaster
Psychic Crusher
Ego Whipper
Mind Thruster

D EFENSE MODES
    Blank Mind
Mind Barrier
Intellectual Fortress
Iron Tower of Will
Shield of Thought (T-Shield)

M INOR DISCIPLINES
    Clairvoyance / Clairaudience
Body Cell Adjustment or Cell Adjust
Etherealness
Invisibility
Telepathy
Telempathic Projector
ESP
Feeblemind

Legend and Lore Reader
Languages
Polymorph Self

MAJOR PSIONIC DISCIPLINES
Body Control
Energy Control
Teleportation
Telekinesis
Shape Changer
Astral Traveller

[Ap-I-4] ACRONYMS and ABBREVIATIONS

DIL - Dionysus Ivy League
Lord HAL - Hero At Large
HOMRA - HAL's Organized Military
Regiment and Academy
HV - Harbor Village
KGB - Kangas Greenbone
GCV - The Great Council of Victory
GCV 705 - GCV Organization
Ratified January 1st, 705
GCV 706 - GCV Organization
Ratified January 1st, 706
NA - The Neutral Alliance
TBH - The Tunnels of Blood / Hell Alliance
TGL - Tarnash - Gindy's Land
of the Far Eastern Dwarves
PC - Player Characters are:
Meşa, Shaman Learus, Kadrah,
Fred G Gearbox, Bannor Son of Barik,
Arion, Isis, Geridan Silverblume,
Salazar, Thundarr, Trinity and Tealini
Doran.
NPC - Non-Player Characters

[Ap-I-5] WIZARD SPELLS
An Extremely Abridged List As Witnessed In Use

JOEY RAULSTON FRED G GEARBOX ULMAETOR
ULRICH ULF UDO URIAH

Charm Person and Charm Monsters
  Dimensional Portal
Magic Jar
Feather Falling or Falling Feather
Cloud of Foul Vapor or Cloud of Stench
Cloud Burst
Fire Ball or Ball of Fire
Fire Wall
Levitation
Lightning Bolt or Bolt of Lightning
Lightning Chain
Image Projection
Object Identification
Object Enchantment
Storm of Ice
Cone of Ice
Polymorph
Polymorph Others
Teleportation - As the Psionic Major
Magic Missiles
Sleep

Swarm of Meteors
Stop Time = Time Stoppage
Stunning Power Word
Limited Wishes
Wish
Shape Changer
Wizard Locking

[Ap-I-6] ILLUSIONIST SPELLS
Another Abridged List As Witnessed In Use

R AULSTON ULMAETOR FRED G GEARBOX SHAMAN LEARUS

S elf Changer
    Self Alteration
Phantasm Force (Options and Upgrades)
Orb of Color
Fascination or Person Fascinate
Monster Fascinate
Fly
Shadow Walking
Improved Phantasmal Force
Invisibility
Mirror Image
Continuous Light or Darkness
Area Hallucination or Land Hallucination
Suggestion
Phantasmagoria
Polymorph Masses
Chaos
Image Projection
Conjure Monsters
True Sight
Tempus Fugit

Illusions of Permanency
Illusions in Program or Program Illusion
Alter Reality
Prismatic Wall / Prismatic Spray

APPENDIX II : The TEXTBOOK of STRATEGIC SHOCK and AWE

By Genoivieve (2nd Edition)

My handbook in its second iteration is rewritten and edited, and I expect its true worth will never be realized by anyone other than high level clerics contemplating effective aggression strategies. Its cost is not insubstantial, and each applicant's motivation to devour the tome must first satisfy my scrutiny.

The contents of this volume are not for the faint of heart. They will be unavailable to those clerics intent on ill purpose. How an ill purpose is defined remains my sole discretion. This is a book designed to augment the profession and does not attempt to proselytize any particular deity alignment or pantheon, but its primary intention must not be evil.

Clerics have never gotten a thorough evaluation and few, if any, outsiders have ever given serious thought to the cleric's aggressive attack possibilities. Everyone assumes a cleric's role is spiritual and nourishing, and of course those principles are fundamental, but at some level of experience clerics need not be limited by such characterization. This is how my prescriptions for *Shock and Awe* establish a new standard.

One deterrent is that clerics cannot muster a lot of attack force at lower ability levels. To be effective, there needs to be a minimum of one top level spell and three second tier spells prepared before any compelling assault can really be entertained. Most give up long before this baseline is achieved, but the relative few who do make it that far are rewarded with unexpected power.

Another problem that continues to raise doubt, albeit an unwarranted doubt that is narrow minded, lies in how spells are interpreted. The majority of cleric spells have a natural, fundamental function that isn't particularly open to any sort of interpretation, but there are some that require an imagination rather more like how an illusionist might employ. Once interpreted and orchestrated in a progressive way, such a spell, and especially strategic spell sequences might be used as effective attacks.

Watch for casting times, ranges, effect zones and spell durations. Spells like WALKING on AIR and CONTINUOUS DARKNESS have generous durations and should be in place long before any combat begins. Shorter duration spells like TRUTH of SIGHT and SPEAKING WITH MONSTERS can be implemented last as the need arises, though as experience is gained, durations obviously become less of a handicap.

Here I want to mention again the power of surprise. Don't ever let them see you coming and never give your target opponent time to think and prepare. This is core to *Strategic Shock and Awe.* If you mess this up, go home and try again later. While your fighter goes in for melee, it is unlikely the opponent will expect anything from you beyond traditional cleric support. This is your advantage.

Watch out for redundancies like WATER WALKING while AIR WALKING, or FINDING TRAPS while TRUE SEEING. Note that combining TONGUES with SPEAKING WITH WHATEVER spells are not redundant. Sometimes you just never know what will work until you try it.

Never underestimate your defenses. Spells such as HEAT, FIRE, COLD, POISON and NEGATIVE MATERIAL PLANE RESISTANCES should be standard fare. AIR WALKING up and out of danger is another obvious out. In all combat situations, at least one and preferably two each of the following spells should be at hand :

WALK on AIR, TRUTH of SIGHT, FLAME BOLT and PLANE SHIFTING

FIRE RESISTANCE, COLD RESISTANCE, NEGATIVE MATERIAL PLANE PROTECTION

At least one each of the following is also required daily whenever possible :

HOLY UTTERANCE, BARRIER OF BLADES, HARM, SPEAKING WITH MONSTERS

DEAD MONSTER ANIMATION, LOWERING WATER, RAISING WATER, CLOUD BURST, DIVINE PREDICTION, CONTINUOUS LIGHT, CONTINUOUS DARKNESS

Strategic spell sequences require more imagination and insight. Alternative interpretations have great potential when premeditated and properly planned.

BARRIER OF BLADES / CONTINUOUS DARKNESS / CONTINUOUS LIGHT / TURN - The Zombie Pizza Sequence

RAISING WATER / CLOUD BURST / WALK on WATER / alt. WALK on AIR - Dungeon Flood Sequence

FIRE RESISTANCE / FLAME BOLT - Army Annihilator Sequence, which can be employed nicely in tandem with :

HOLY UTTERANCE / HARM / SPEAKING WITH MONSTERS - The Subduction Sequence

This powerful spell sequence was composed and beta tested to good effect at the Hill Giants immediately east of the Great Bog and The Druid Stronghold.

AERIAL ATTENDANT PARADE / QUEST PARADE / PROTECTION FROM EVIL 10' R / FONT SCRY PARADE / DIETY COMMUNE - Home Front Orchestra

NEGATIVE MATERIAL PLANE PROTECTION / WALK ON AIR / TURN then PLANE SHIFTING then HOLY UTTERANCE - Ghost Surprise Sequence

MEŞA's MAGNIFICENT WIELD - Secret Proprietary Weapon Spell

SEISMIC INFUSION then OBJECT ANIMATION - Missiles can be produced from the rubble.

DEVIL EXACTION / HOLY UTTERANCE / DIETY GATE - Forced Attraction Sequence

OBJECT LOCATION / LOWERING WATER / FINDING THE PATH / FINDING TRAPS / alt. TRUTH of SIGHT - Treasure Seeker Sequence

APPENDIX III : WORLD ESTABLISHMENT

Hellenistic Pantheons In Worship of the Following Gods :
Athena Apollo Aphrodite Ares Dionysus Hera Hades Poseidon and Zeus

---

ATHENA - DEMETER
Father Elitch Leipzig Callan

Grand GCV Patriarch

Kalaringus Tell GCV

Lord Aisodon GCV

Bahamut GCV

Salazar Doran PC Patriarch

and Doran PC residents Lord Trinity, Tealini Doran and Geridan Silverblume

Havtovalla, Lord Gray Fulton III and Calefangor were assassinated by TBH.

A PHRODITE

Genoivieve - Milan GCV

Grand Matriarch

Lord HAL GCV

Meşa - Sodon Calamy PC GCV Matriarch

Vanita - Harbor Village Matriarch

Ren - Fered Calamy Matriarch

Cal - Milan (dual-classed) Patriarch

Aneas - Fered Soudron (dual-classed)

Also acolytes Jordan (HOMRA dual-classed), Teresa, Oline and Nicky-Meline (dual classed) in Fered Calamy, Sabrina and Gianna in Milan, Norma Jean and Danny (dual-classed) in Harbor Village, and Amery (dual classed) in Fered Soudron.

A POLLO

St. Bodan - Milan GCV Patriarch

Grand Apollo Patriarch

Burk - Fered Loron Milan GCV Patriarch

Marshall Kesselring GCV Associate

Bannor son of Barik, Ranger

Arion, Ranger

Boddart - Milan

Bilban - Fered Loron

Z EUS

Sandon - Stronghold GCV Patriarch

Grand Patriarch and Chairman

Falin of Tarnash GCV

Numencön of GL - Retired

Sir Greenway - Retiring

Isis - Sandon's Stronghold
Fered Soudron PC Matriarch

H ADES
Roxy - Ersa Calamy Matriarch and
Grand Matriarch of Hades
Layla - Sodon Calamy Matriarch
Lorelei - Hades Matriarch Title Revoked
Lydia
Livia
Ulmaetor Ulrich Ulf Udo and Uriah

D IONYSUS and THE NEUTRAL ALLIANCE
The Vortex - Ersa Calamy Chairman and
Grand Patriarch
Karim - Sovan Cunard Patriarch
Vespertine - Sodon Calamy Patriarch
and all NA Members including Kadrah the Hierophant (PC), The
Kastovina Brothers, Shaman Learus (PC), Fred G. Gearbox (PC),
Sir Daniel The Grand Druid and Borg. Initially Raulston and Ulmer
were firmly in this alignment before things went sour. Note also that
the important fact that Druids are not technically aligned, but remain
closely connected to the NA.

H ERA-ARTEMIS POSEIDON ARES
These gods are represented in parts of the World not
associated with this story, but nevertheless exit somewhere in the
distant East.

APPENDIX IV : GCV Successional Timeline

THE GCV 703 - 5 Core 6 Associates
Members - Sandon, Falin - ZEUS
5 Aisodon, Joey, Bahamut
ATHENA-DEMETER
Associates - Kesselring, St. Bodan
6 Greenway, Numencrön
Genoivieve, Father Elitch
July 28, 703 BIENNIAL SUMMIT -
Meşa's Proposition
St. Bodan, Genoivieve, Elitch,
Burk are appointed as
Numencrön Retires.
(5-5)

Jan 1, 704 (5-5) Status Quo - No Change
July 28, 704 INFORMAL FIRST ANNUAL
SUMMIT - Status Quo (5-5)
Jan 1, 705 - THE GCV 705 -
St. Bodan and Burk,

Genoivieve and Elitch
ascend to Full Membership.
Kesselring and Greenway
remain as Interim Associates.
THE GCV 705 is established.
9 Core 2 Associates (9-2)

The GCV 706 and Its Final Stages of Evolution

July 28, 705 BIENNIAL SUMMIT -
Meşa, HAL and Kesselring are
appointed for Ascension to Full
Membership.
9 Core 2 Associates
Jan 1, 706 Meşa, HAL and Kesselring
ascend to Full Membership.
Greenway retires and the
Associate Membership is
dissolved. GCV has 12 Core
Members.
12 Core 0 Associates

Annual Grand Summit
on July 28, 705
GCV Inauguration Ceremony

on January 1, 706

CORE MEMBERSHIP = 12

ZEUS - Sandon - Chairman
    with both Veto and
the Tie Breaker Vote - 56th Level
King Falin 52
ATHENA-DEMETER -
Father Elitch 45
Joey (Demeter Only) 27
Lord Aisodon 27
Bahamut
APOLLO - St. Bodan 30
Burk 19
Field Marshall Kesselring 26
APHRODITE - Genoivieve 35
Ninmeşaora 22
Lord HAL 22

APPENDIX V : MAPS IMAGES and Bibliography

TSR Inc. Lake Geneva, Wisconsin
Later Wizards On The Coast Ltd.

Advanced Dungeons & Dragons
The Dungeon Master's Guide
The Player's Handbook
Unearthed Arcana
The Monster Manual
The Monster Manual II
Fiend Folio
Legends & Lore
Manual of the Planes

Most Advanced Dungeons & Dragons literature was invented and written by Gary Gygax, the Grandfather of the Role Playing Game Concept.

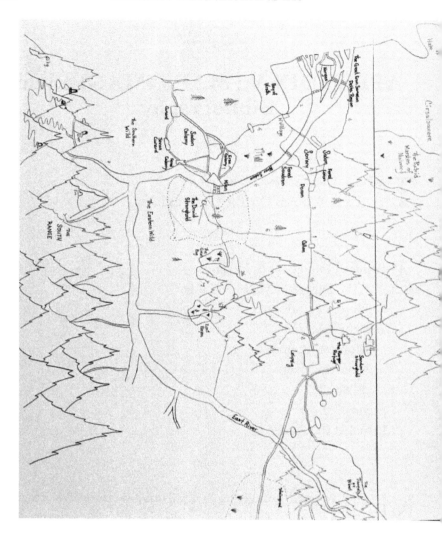

THE KNOWN WORLD WEST

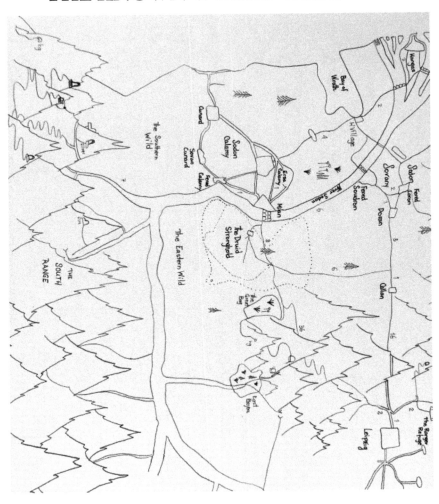

THE WORLD WEST MAGNIFIED

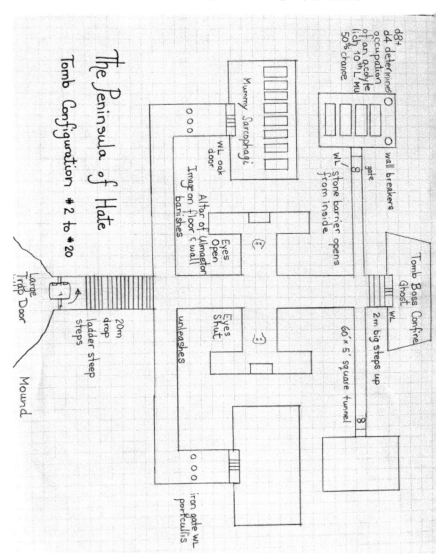

The Peninsula of Hate

Tomb Configuration #2 to #20

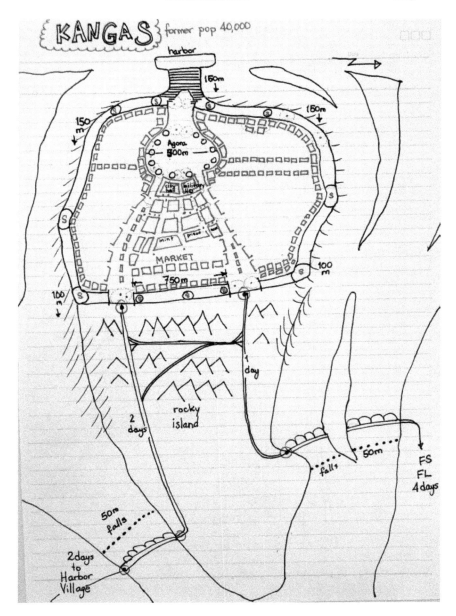

KANGAS former pop 40,000

harbor

150m

150m

150m

Agora
500m

city military
hall bldg

mint prison

MARKET

750m

100 m

100 m

1 day

2 days

rocky island

50m falls

FS FL 4 days

50m falls

2 days to Harbor Village

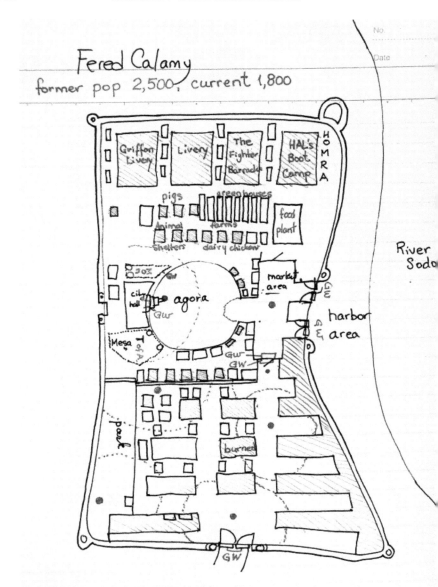

Fered Calamy
former pop 2,500, current 1,800

Don't miss out!

Visit the website below and you can sign up to receive emails whenever Martin Werner Zander publishes a new book. There's no charge and no obligation.

https://books2read.com/r/B-A-MXUAB-BLSDD

BOOKS 2 READ

Connecting independent readers to independent writers.

Did you love *Ulmaetor*? Then you should read *Genoivieve*[1] by Martin Werner Zander!

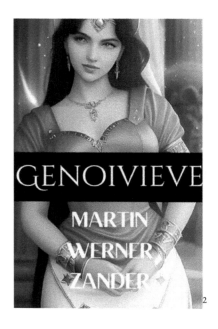

[2]

Plunge head first into an epic journey of courage and fortune with *Genoivieve,* a captivating high fantasy novel that places you inside a complex world filled with magic and intrigue. In this charming tale, you live the extraordinary life of Genoivieve, a human Cleric of Aphrodite, as she navigates the immersive landscape of a once peaceful and prosperous realm suddenly subjugated by extreme evil.

Genoivieve is not only a powerful Cleric of Aphrodite. She represents resilience and honor, demonstrating a unique goodness that inspires. As she deals with her own inner demons and engages various overlapping forces of darkness, Genoivieve discovers that her destiny is intricately linked to the world. While embracing traditional themes

1. https://books2read.com/u/mKVZoB

2. https://books2read.com/u/mKVZoB

of love, trust and integrity, she defies societal expectations, eliminating barriers designed to confine women.

Encountering intense danger and great personal risk, Genoivieve's unwavering faith and determination empower dozens of interesting characters around her, qualifying the notion that leadership and strength are not a function of gender. It happens in a setting where females are generally suppressed but blatant misogyny, racism and homophobia are not widespread prejudices. *Genoivieve* therefore makes a strong case for an increased female readership in a genre that has historically been male-oriented.

With expertly-crafted world building and a compelling, first-person narrative, *Genoivieve* is a mesmerizing tale delightfully accented with hints of allegory and literary nuance. No AI was employed in the written word or any hand-drawn maps. The story provides a genuine mosaic of classical legend and lore, ideal for all fans of high fantasy, contemporary fantasy and sword & sorcery role-playing alike, and represents a fine read within the genre.

Also by Martin Werner Zander

Genoivieve
Genoivieve
Ulmaetor

About the Author

The inspiration for this writing journey began in sunny, southern British Columbia almost 45 years ago. As a classical, pencil-and-paper Dungeon Master forever in demand, my D&D game continues in Japan with new player characters eager to improvise and develop their own stories. New players are millennials who add a real freshness to D&D with their inclination towards modern society themes and the use of contemporary language. Together with our 1980s-era, old-school, Canadian players championing this effort, all kinds of amazing adventures playing out over the years have found their way into these books.

I hope you'll have as much fun with Genoivieve and Ulmaetor as I have had, developing characters and writing about the world through their experiences. It happens in a setting where women are generally suppressed but blatant misogyny, racism and homophobia are not widespread prejudices. In particular, as I applaud women for generally reading more, Genoivieve makes a case for an increased female readership in a genre that has historically been male-oriented.

The content of these contemporary high fantasies is influenced by JRR Tolkien, Gary Gygax, RA Salvatore, Robert E Howard and a tiny dollop of Charles Dickens, so if you're familiar with the celebrated masterpieces from any of these ground-breaking authors, we already have something in common. Eternal gratitude goes to all my veteran players for their suggestions and support, and to my darling soulmate Yoko, without whom the endless nights spent proofreading might have been overwhelming!

Apart from writing and conducting my ongoing RPG, my day job is operating an English school in Japan. I'm an avid vintage record collecter of various genres and play music every day, often quite loud! Yoko and I love traveling to the Mediterranean region to inspect classical historical monuments. A deeper insight into the ancient Hellenistic and Roman world has proven useful. Other major hobby passions include visual astronomy, freediving and photography. I can really get mired into anything involving optics. Although age and the Pandemic have naturally caused some skills to decline, the silver lining is that I did find more time to write! Therefore stay tuned for more in the future!

With My Very Best Wishes and Sincere Thanks,
MARTIN WERNER ZANDER